HENRY

THE SWAMP DOCTOR

HENRY

THE SWAMP DOCTOR

Ethel M.T. Bailey

AuthorHouse™
1663 Liberty Drive
Bloomington, IN 47403
www.authorhouse.com
Phone: 1 (800) 839-8640

Published by AuthorHouse 06/24/2015

ISBN: 978-1-5049-1758-2 (sc)
ISBN: 978-1-5049-1757-5 (hc)
ISBN: 978-1-5049-1756-8 (e)

Library of Congress Control Number: 2015909602

Print information available on the last page.

This book is printed on acid-free paper.

Henry, the Swamp Doctor
By: Ethel M.T. Bailey

This book is dedicated to my long suffering family and friends.

My children: Donna & Warren, Kim & Ken
My grandchildren: Christian, Michael, Andy,
Ashley, Justin, Jason and Dylan
My great-grandchildren:
Madeline, Annabella, Noah, Aiden, Stevie Ray,
Talan, Ellison, Lynden, and Gretchen

My long-time friends: Jay & Melissa M. and their grandson Joshua

Special thanks to my friend Sandy Josey for her editing skills.

Contents

ILLUSTRATION CREDITS

Chapter One:
"Henry" (author's personal photograph)
"Idle Wile" (original name: "Destrehan Plantation" by Connie Hanna)
"Justice" (author's personal photograph)

Chapter Two:
"Charlie" (photography by Tim Garlington)
"Mooney" (author's personal photograph)
"Lantern" (author's personal photograph)

Chapter Three:
"Indian with Bow" (istockphoto.com)

Chapter Four:
"Lil' Wolf" (istockphoto.com

Chapter Six:
"Marie Laveau" (istockphoto.com)
"Father Jerome" (istockphoto.com)

Chapter Seven:
"Ms. Kay's House" (original name: "Rienzi Plantation" by Martin Beniot)

Chapter Eight:
"Cafe du Monde" (original name "Landmarks of the Quarter" by Martin Beniot)
"Parade Float" (original name "Mardi Gras Scenes" by Martin Benoit)
"Charlie's House" (original name "Madewood" by Martin Beniot)

Chapter Nine:
"Charlie and Ben Fishing" (by Wendell G. Williamson)
"Mosquito Hawk" (istockphoto.com)
"Josh" (personal photograph from Jay Melancon)
"Boats" (author's original artwork)

Chapter Ten
"The Harvest" (original name "Cotton Pickin' Time" by Martin Benoit)

Chapter Thirteen
"Fire on the River" (original name "Levee Bonfires" by Martin Benoit)

Chapter Fifteen
"Luggage Wagon" (original name "Tour of the Quarter" by Martin Benoit)

Chapter Sixteen
"Duck on the Water" (by Wendell G. Williamson)
"Deer in the Woods" (by Wendell G. Williamson)

Chapter Seventeen
"The Street Car" (original name "The St. Charles Line" by Martin Benoit)

Chapter Eighteen
"St. Louis Cathedral" (by Martin Benoit)

Chapter Nineteen
"Maiden of the Stars" (istockphoto.com)

Character List

Main Characters	Relationship to Henry	Home
Henry Noah Arrington		Idle Wile' Plantation
Charles "Charlie" Williams	Friend	The Shadows Plantation
Josh P. Melancon	Nephew	Idle Wile' Plantation
Amy M. Arrington	Mother	Idle Wile' Plantation
Noah Arrington	Brother	Idle Wile' Plantation
Ben Arrington	Brother	Idle Wile' Plantation
Madeline and Bella	Sisters	Idle Wile' Plantation
Bud Arrington	Uncle	Wild Acres Plantation
IJ Arrington	Uncle	Twin Oaks Plantation
Jimmie Arrington	Uncle	Magnolia Plantation
Dr. & Jane Francis Grant	Sister & brother-in-law	The Myrtles Plantation
Mr. & Mrs. Charles Williams I	Charlie's mother and father	Golden Ridge Plantation
Katherine Kurts "Mrs. K"	Friend	Moon Glow Plantation
el Rico	Butler	Idle Wile' Plantation
Ms. Bessie	Cook	Idle Wile' Plantation
Sassy	Servant	Idle Wile' Plantation
Willie G.	Gardener	Idle Wile' Plantation
Lil' Wolf	Friend	Chitimacha Indian Tribe
Jean Lafitte	Pirate	the ship Jolly Roger
Marie Laveau	Voodoo Queen	New Orleans, Louisiana

Introduction

The State of Louisiana had ten European countries claiming it as a territory in the early years of its settlement.

France, Spain, and England were three of the countries to fly their flags over Louisiana for a period of time in the history of our country.

This story is fiction. It's a story of a Louisiana man named Henry who inherits his father's property after his sudden death. The property of twenty–thousand acres of prime Louisiana land is located along the banks of the muddy Mississippi River. This large piece of land was located above the city of New Orleans, known as the Queen City of the South: a city worth fighting over.

The twenty-thousand acres of land was awarded to Gustave Arrington by the Queen of France for services rendered during the battle between Spain and France over the City of New Orleans.

Gustave divided the land into five large farms, known as "plantations" in Louisiana, for his family. The land was divided into the main Louisiana crops of sugar cane, corn, beets, rice, and cotton fields. Some of the land was planted in vegetables, fruit, and pecan trees.

This is their story along with their families, friends, and foes.

I hope you enjoy living in this story as you read it, as much as I did as I wrote it.

Thank you,
Ethel M. T. Bailey, Author

Chapter One

"DAWN"

Bailey, Ethel M. T.

Henry could still see the misty swirls of the fog flirting in and around the gray moss that hung from the old oak trees of the forest. It was very early in the morning, the best time of the day. It was just before dawn and the forest was so quiet you could hear the water lapping as it met the shore of the Bayou.

Henry stooped down by the waters' edge to trickle the clear water through his fingers. He could feel the coolness of the morning.

He filled his cheeks with air to make a chuckling sound from his throat like the gray squirrels. Then Henry was very quiet; stillness filled the forest.

A low chuckling sound was repeated coming from a branch above Henry's head. A gray squirrel joined in Henry's song of the forest. Henry grinned as he recognized the chuckling sound from one of the wild animals he loved best.

Dawn was breaking in the East as Henry leaned back on a tree by the bayou and chewed on a stick. He was waiting for the sun to rise over the waters' edge. Its golden oval globe of fire woke the forest and farm animals alike. The long-tail squirrel waited, too. Blue Jays were beginning to chirp in the trees and a turtle came out from the grass and leaves to drink at the water's edge.

Pretty soon the family of blue jay's approached the water. They tested the water and checked the surrounding forest. They drank deeply of the cool water then they flopped and flapped and splashed the water all over their feathers for their morning bath.

When they returned to the bank they flew up to a tall tree branch and shook themselves dry. They picked each feather with their beaks to clean them. Then they flew down to the forest floor to dance in the early morning light and look for bugs and things to eat.

Henry jumped up as something hit his shoulder hard and gripped it. He was startled and he grabbed the little hand that grasped him.

"Josh, don't do that son, you could get shot that way!" exclaimed Henry.

"Uncle Henry, I thought you heard me and you couldn't shoot anything while you have the Rosary clinched in your hand," said a sorry Josh for sneaking up on Henry.

"Josh, you are as quiet as a lizard in the woods," laughed Henry, as he watched Josh's face turn red at this remark.

"How did you find me at such an early hour - just at sunrise - in the woods?" Asked Henry, wondering why Josh was up so early today. It was barely daylight.

"I woke up this morning and remembered that I will be baptized pretty soon and I am not sure I will be ready. I heard you leave the house and I decided to come and talk to you about the Catechism and prayers I need to learn before I can receive The Holy Sacraments at Christmas time." explained Josh.

"Josh," replied Henry, "I didn't forget about your Baptism on Christmas Eve. We will be ready, I promise. You only need to know if you want to become a Catholic. That is the only question Father Jerry will ask you for your Baptism. You say the Rosary with Mom and the girls before going to bed every night. You know those prayers. I promise you Josh, you are ready now to become Catholic like the rest of the family. We are just waiting for the Ceremony."

"All our family and friends will be at Mid-night Mass for the celebration of the Birth of Baby Jesus. It will be a special night for the Baby Jesus and you, Josh. It will be a big day for all of us. We will be in New Orleans for Christmas and Father will say Mass in the beautiful St. Louis Cathedral on Christmas Eve. I promise you, we will have a big dinner with cake and ice cream afterwards."

"Yes!" shouted Josh, "And the next day is Christmas! Santa Clause is coming to town!" sang a happy Joshua. "Not to mention presents under the Christmas Tree."

"Oh yes" Laughed Henry. 'Good! We have a very happy boy.' he thought.

"Look up, Josh" said Henry.

Josh was amazed to see the sky growing brighter with the rising sun. The stars were beginning to fade but their sparkle still dusted the early morning sky. The sun was rising from the East; a big ball of fire. Daybreak was slowly crossing over the blue waters of the Bayou.

The big silver full moon was dancing it's way across the sky to set in the Western skyline once again. It will rise again from the East to shine once more on the Earth for another southern night of delight over the waters of the Bayou Teche'.

The big Oak trees were filtering the sunlight turning the trees and leaves into golden colors throughout the forest. There were colors of yellow, green, scarlet, reds, and orange to mention a few. These are the beautiful exciting wonders of God and Nature.

Henry crept to the edge of the water for a cool drink while wily squirrels checked their domain of the woods and kept watch over Henry's progress to the waters' edge.

When Henry finished drinking, he took Josh by the hand and said, "O.K. Josh, let's start your lessons now as we walk back to the house for breakfast."

"How?" asked Josh, puzzled and looking up at his Uncle Henry walking beside him.

"Look around you, Josh." smiled Henry. "God is here now. God made the world and all that is in it. He made all things, seen and unseen. He is The Most Powerful and All Good and Loving. See, that is your first lesson." smiled Henry, watching Josh's face light up with a smile.

"Learn it, remember it, and we will take it from there. Later as we spend time together you will learn more. You will also learn from the people around you. They also follow in "The Footsteps of God". They all love you."

"All the people around you, love you, Josh. They take care of you and watch over you in His name. They Love you as God teaches us in the fourth Commandment, 'Love Thy Neighbor as Thy self.' That's you and me and all of us, and we follow it every day, all day." finished Henry.

"Wow and, wow!" said Josh. "You sure know how to teach, Uncle Henry."

"It's easy Josh." said Henry. "God is Love and I love God and I Love You."

"Why do you have your Rosary with you in the woods?" asked Josh watching Uncle Henry put his Rosary in a little leather pouch and then drop it in his watch pocket.

Looking down at his hands, Henry said, "You know Josh, it's my time to talk to God and listen to Him. I also pray to His Mother, Mary. I get so busy during the day I'm afraid I will forget to thank Jesus for His many gifts He has given our family and friends. And that is not a good thing Josh, as you know.

"Yes, that's what I learned from you Uncle Henry and I want to be baptized on Christmas Eve and you will be my Godfather, right?" asked a serious Josh.

"Yes, Josh." said Henry.

"I need you to take me to Catechism class after Mass with Father Jerry and the Nuns or I won't be ready to answer the questions for the test." frowned Josh.

"The lessons start this Sunday after Mass and I promise you, you will be ready for Father to give you the test on the lessons you have learned. After all Josh, you have been going to Mass with Mom and me for over a year now. You know how to say the Rosary and make the Sign of the Cross. You say all the prayers with Mom, Noah, and the girls every night. You will pass with flying colors. And we will celebrate your Baptism after Mass with **everyone."** promised Henry.

Josh had lost his parents, Henry's sister Jane and her husband John, in an accident in Africa where they lived. Catholic Churches were rare and far between from their Ranch. Josh had not been baptized in Africa.

Henry and his Mother Amy went to get Josh who was very young. He had made his home with his Grandmother Amy and Uncle Henry ever since.

Josh was happy living on Idle Wile' Plantation with cousins, aunts, uncles, and friends living all around him.

Idle Wile

"Henry! Henry Josh! Where are you? Breakfast is ready and you have been in the woods an extra- long time this morning. Ms. Bessie is waiting for you; she needs to get on with your meal. Hurry up! Hurry up!" called Amy, looking toward the woods waiting for Henry and Josh to emerge from the forest.

Henry and Josh came from the woods just as Amy, Henry's Mother (and Josh's Grandmother), came to the edge of the lawn of Idle Wile' Plantation where they all lived, worked, laughed, and prayed each day.

"Henry, why have you and Josh been so long in the woods this morning?" asked a puzzled Amy.

"Well Mom, Josh came to meet me early this morning to talk to me about his Baptism and First Communion. I think he is a little worried that he will not be ready for these two Sacraments of the Church." explained Henry, as he took Amy's hand and walked across the lawn to the screen door of the back porch of the family's mansion.

"Come, come, Josh, you and Henry can wash up and come to the kitchen for breakfast," said Amy, as she hurried Henry and Josh into the bathroom to clean up for breakfast.

Henry and Josh came into the kitchen and approached the big table covered with a white table cloth with a napkin at each place setting for the family's first meal of the day.

"Good Morning, Ms Bessie and Sassy, we are so sorry for being late for breakfast. Josh and I got to talking at the water's edge this morning. The animals and birds were so busy in the forest, we watched them for a while. We forgot the passing of time" apologized Henry, with Josh by his side.

"Now, now, Mr. Henry, we don't worry 'bout you and Josh! We know you coming in for breakfast as soon as you get too hungry to stay in the woods with the animals because we know they are eating bugs and such and you and Josh don't eat all those kinda things. We not worried." said Ms Bessie.

Ms Bessie and Sassy grinned at Henry and Josh as they pulled out their chairs to sit at the table that was filled with bowls of grits, syrup, hot biscuits, jam, jellies, and butter. Yummy.

"Yes, yes" frowned Amy, "We all know you two have spoiled these boys something awful. Spoiled rotten, is how you have them." frowned Amy, some more.

Madeline, Noah, and Bella came in snickering about Henry and Josh getting corrected by Mom for delaying breakfast this morning for everyone else.

"Yes Ma'am, Ms. Amy. Me and Sassy know we got them spoiled rotten, that's right, huh Sassy?" laughed Ms Bessie, eying Sassy, who was hiding her smile behind her white apron.

"Yes, Ma'am," said Sassy, on her way to look for Ben, the youngest of the boys, who was still missing for breakfast. Ms Bessie started breaking eggs to fry to complete the meal while waiting for Ben.

Amy looked at the children and asked, "just where is Ben?" Noah shook his head,he did not know where Ben was this morning.

Henry looked around the kitchen again and said, "Where is our Lazy Bones, Benjamin this morning," he frowned.

"I'm here, Henry. I am so sorry for being so late. I couldn't find my boots this morning. I put them on the porch last night to clean this morning. They were full of 'Yuk and Yuk' from the pasture. I was going to clean them early this morning but when I looked for them where I left them last night, they were gone. I was looking all over the porch and steps for them," frowned Ben.

"Well, little boy, I bet someone picked them up while you were sleeping and cleaned all the 'Yuk and Yuk' off them," laughed Henry.

"I know, I know. I thanked Emma profusely and sincerely for cleaning my yucky boots," said a serious Ben.

"Well that's good Ben, because Emma had to take them out into the back yard to clean them with brushes and rags. I know how she cleans all of our yucky boots. We need to get her a treat; in fact, we can add Ms Bessie and Sassy's' names for treats from town when we go to get feed and other things we need." said Henry as he remembered all the things the ladies of the house did for them in their care of them all.

"Thank you, Mr. Henry, we sure appreciate it," said Bessie, watching Sassy and Emma smiling at each other, wondering what kind of treat Mr. Henry would be getting for them.

Amy was watching the ladies and Henry, wondering just what kind of threat he was thinking of. Nice material for new church dresses would be nice. With new gloves she knew they needed and shoes would also be nice. She was making a list in her head to pin to Henrys' lapel when he went into town to shop for the farms and the 'ladies'.

Henry asked everyone to bow their heads for the blessing to thank God for all the blessings He bestowed on his family and friends.

After the blessing, Ms Bessie filled the coffee cups and the milk glasses for the family.

Everyone was eating the delicious breakfast when there was a knock on the screen door. Jerome, the Manager of all five Arrington Plantations, as well as Idle Wile's Foreman, came into the kitchen.

"Good Morning, Jerome," said Henry as he stood up to shake hands with his friend and foreman as Jerome took off his hat.

"Ms Bessie, please get Jerome a cup of coffee," said Amy as she looked at Jerome to see if there was trouble around the property.

"Thank you, Ms. Amy," said Jerome, "I sure can use one. We have trouble with the cattle, dairy cows, and calf stock."

"Sit down, Jerome." said Henry as he pulled out a chair.

Ms Bessie handed Jerome a fresh strong hot, sweet, cup of coffee.

"Thank you, Ms Bessie" said a worried looking Jerome.

As Jerome sipped his coffee, Henry waited for him to speak of whatever was bothering him this morning.

"What's going on, Jerome?" asked Henry.

"Well, Mr. H., the dairy cows, cattle, and calves are all missing this morning. The gate to the barn was found open and the field fence was trampled down. The herd is all missing, but we have a lot of tracks to follow. I wanted to come and tell you as soon as possible so we could get started to look for them and find whoever is responsible for this problem. I sent a messenger to the other farms to let your uncles know about the missing herd," Explained Jerome.

"Don't worry Jerome, we have had trouble before now and we always managed to find out the truth and fix the problem in a few hours," said Henry as he got up from the table and grabbed his hat to go outside.

"I think I hear Uncle Jimmy, Bud, and I.J.'s voices in the barnyard now. Ms Bessie, please fix Jerome a plate of your delicious breakfast while I go talk to the Uncles." said Henry.

"Mom, I think the children should stay near the house with you and Mitch in case we have a big problem with rustlers' or other trouble makers today. Ben, Noah, Josh, stay around the house where Mom and Mr. Mitch can keep an eye on you. Girls, I know you will be at Aunt Susan's house, so you will be inside with the cousins and safe. Anyone who steals cows will take children too. O.K. boys?" asked Henry.

"Yes, Uncle Henry, we will be fine at home today. The cousins are coming to spend the day with me, Noah, and Ben. They are always fun and they help with the chores." said Josh.

I.J., Jim, and Bud were already in the barn yard with their horses, Princess and Dakota. Princess, Buds' horse, was beautiful, and as Bud liked to say, she was a race horse. Princess was a powerful racing machine. She would race with anything and all things on four legs or two. She won in every competition. Princess would prance and paw the ground, in hopeful anticipation of a competitor.

Dakota, I.J.'s horse, was a Palomino with a blonde mane, tail, and body. I.J would always brag on Dakota's strength and swiftness. Dakota was thrown together with Princess in all local races and won his share of prizes. The local horses did not have a chance of winning against these two prize horses of the Arrington family.

It was a well-known fact that the mayor of St. Mary Parish, Chris Hanks, would inform all new people moving into the area, "Do not bet your hard earned money against Dakota or Princess in a racing competition.

You, my friend, will lose every time; even in fun." Chris would laugh. He had learned by experience

"St. Mary Parish politicians," Henry would declare, as he watched his friend light his cigar while keeping his eye on Henry and the Uncles, "were always looking out for the benefit of our reputation as good, honest citizens."

"The mayor is afraid we scare away the citizens who are settling in his Parish to leave and move to another less intimidating town, or even worse yet, another parish out of his jurisdiction!" Teased I.J.

I.J. and the family knew that Mayor Chris, a good friend, had a good sense of humor even if the joke was at his expense.

"O.K., O.K.," laughed Chris, "I will be sure and take care of our new people and you."

I.J. and Bud were waiting for Henry and Jerome to meet them in the back yard. The horses were getting impatient. Dakota was pawing the ground in frustration; he was not good at waiting.

"O.K. Dakota, take it easy, you are not in control, sir." laughed I.J. who was always in control of everything in his vicinity, he hoped.

The screen door opened and Henry stepped down the back steps to meet his Uncles.

"Good Morning Uncles, I am so sorry about the news of the missing animals this morning. Not good news for a Monday morning or any morning, in fact." He said as he shook hands with each Uncle in turn.

"What do you think could have happened to them?" asked Henry.

"Rustlers," said Bud. "I saw the Sheriff yesterday and he said he saw several rough looking strangers in town. They looked like they didn't know anyone in town and they were buying buck shot for their shot guns."

"Well, you may be right Uncle, but there may be another villain we all know in these parts." said Henry. "I know for a fact, that Jean Lafitte put his ships into the little Bay of St. Helena just day before yesterday. I just wonder if there is a connection between that bad bandit landing there and our prize dairy herd missing today."

"Jean Lafitte is now landing in St. Helena Bay to bury his stolen loot. That notorious pirate of Louisiana steals from any foreign galleons he can fool by flying the British Flag and then changing to his true colors of the Black and White Flag with **the SKULL AND CROSS BONES;** his true nature and occupation." frowned Henry, while watching the faces of the others to see if they agreed with his description of the Pirate Jean Lafitte.

Jean Lafitte was well known in the French Quarters and in Jackson Square of New Orleans as well. There is a famous alley in New Orleans, between the Saint Louis Cathedral and the famous Pontalba Building. This alley measures about seventeen or twenty feet between the two buildings and is known as Pirate's Alley. This is where Jean Lafitte makes his famous sales of the treasures he loots from ships at sea.

The Mounted Police of New Orleans have also made this alley famous by tracking down Jean Lafitte and his merry-wily crew of lawless men of misadventure that made him famous in Louisiana and throughout the world.

This history of Jean Lafitte and his wily crew of henchmen was well known to the Arrington Family and their neighbors and friends. Lafitte landed his ships just five or six miles from the Arrington Plantations and other in that area of the Parish.

"Lafitte is well known for liquoring up the Biloxi Indian Tribe to do his dirty work of digging holes all over St. Helena Island to bury his stolen treasure. He has looted from the Spanish, British, and any other boats he can board with hooks and chains to kill and plunder for the treasure they are carrying." added Henry.

"Then he runs to hide around the islands bordering the seas and the rivers along his route. Only France is safe from his plundering since France is his home country."

"Lafitte's men are too tired and home sick to dig in the dirt for Lafitte. But the Indians do it willingly for the liquor and trinkets he gives them. They are too liquored up to remember where they buried the Treasure and too afraid of the Pirate to go look." finished Henry.

"Yes," said Uncle Jimmie, "You are so right Henry. But what do you propose we do now?" He asked.

"Well," said Henry, "Jerome will lead us down one trail from the Plantation to where he thinks the thieves have driven the cattle away from the homestead. So we are taking ten men from the farm to help find the herd and drive them home."

"In another case," continued Henry, "If the cattle have been stolen, we have plenty enough men and guns to take care of the bandits and hold them captive until the Sheriff gets here. Then we can re-capture the herd and drive them home."

So, here is Jerome and the cattlemen, ready to pursue this plan. Jerome and ten men on horseback came into the yard ready to take orders to hunt for the lost herd.

"O.K., Mr. H.," said Jerome as he came into the yard, "We are ready to go."

"Well, lets' start in the upper pastures where the grass is long and the cows will graze and the thieves, whoever they are, will think they can hide behind the trees and bushes," said I.J., the lawyer and reader of many books on the habits of livestock and criminals alike. The brothers all agreed, and Henry, who is always in control.

"If that plan fails, I think we ought to check the bayou. The animals will always find the cool water on a hot day like today," said Jerome.

The men were ready to take care of any and all problems that may crop up. They were mounted on strong horses and were well equipped with leather whips, guns, and rifles in case of trouble. Everyone had a 'Don't mess with us' attitude on their faces.

The men had traveled hard for about three miles when Jerome started fussing and pulled-up on Thunders' bridle hard to stop him in his tracks.

"Jerome?" said Henry as he pulled Justice close to the other horse with Jimmy, I.J. and Bud not far behind. Jerome watched Henry come close to him and, almost in a whisper, Jerome started explaining to the men beside him of the problem that he noticed on the trail they had taken. The other men came to a stop at a signal from Jerome to be quiet and to quieten the horses down.

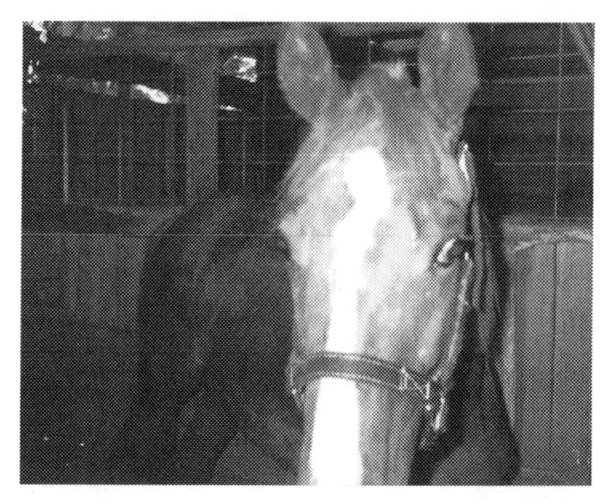

Justice

Jerome explained, "The trail shows that the herd has leveled the grass on each side of the main path to a depth of three feet on each side. I think they have gone, or were driven, too near to the corn fields that are almost mature enough to harvest. If my thinking is correct, then the cattle might be in the corn field. Mr. Henry, we must be very quiet and slow our horses down not to scare and stampede the cattle. They will destroy the crop in no time at all." whispered Jerome.

"Jerome, you lead," said Henry, "we will follow your lead. Does everyone understand what Jerome is saying, how this effort to 'round-up' the stray cattle and slowly move them out of the corn field is the only way to save the crop of corn that has been planted by the five family plantations? This is the 'Cash Crop' of the families for the year. We'll see if they are there."

"Oh no!" said I.J. "This is a disaster".

"Uncle, maybe they are not in the corn field. Jerome just wants us to be prepared before we get there to be quiet and keep the horses under control and quiet, so we are prepared to gently round up the cattle to drive them from the field without too much damage to the corn." explained Henry.

"Mr. Henry, we need Joe here to be on watch for any men or Indians that may have driven the cattle here. We may not be clear of that element, yet." said Jerome.

"Good idea Jerome, we will follow your lead." agreed Henry.

Jerome then turned his horse to the west of the trail and Henry and the men followed his lead. The group went quietly up the trail after Jerome.

"Oh no," Said Bud as they came near to the track the cattle had taken right into the corn field. The cows were munching and trampling many acres of crop under their big hoofs.

"If they keep on eating, they will suffer from stomach cramps and some will die." warned I.J. They then quietly and gently herded the cattle into a bunch and drove them through the field that had been trampled, hardly hurting the remaining stalks of corn that could be harvested in a few days as soon as the trampled corn could be cleaned out of the way and the fields made ready for the harvest.

The farmers were just in time to save most of the fields of corn and to realize in those moments, that with hard work the 'Cash Crop' would survive to help them all.

The men slowly rounded up the dairy cows that were docile in nature. The calves followed their Mama's and then the heifers. The men were calmly walking their horses alongside and behind the herd.

Uncle Bud started humming an old French song he had learned as a young boy on Paw Paw's Farm in New Iberia, one of the oldest Plantations in that area. The home was named 'White House Plantation'. This song's lyrics were sung by Mamas to their babies to put them to sleep.

It went like this:

Fe Do, Do, Cher' tète Fia or Garson' aw Mom's – Go to Sleep, dear little girl or boy of Moms'. He had learned this little French song in conversation when his family spoke. The French Language was learned at home and was taught in The Convent by the Sister's (Nun's) from France.

Bud hummed the cattle into complete submission so the round-up, performed by the men and horses of the farms, could be done quietly and gently.

Soon they reached the cow pens of the farm and the horsemen walked the cattle and heifers into the fenced in area. Whistling and circling their whips over the cattle's heads leading the herd into the fenced in area where they belonged. The men quickly locked and double locked the gates as they secured the cattle in their area. No more of that nonsense.

Bud hummed the dairy cows and calves into the barn where the dairy workers were ready to clean the cows to be milked. It was very late in the day for this first milking. That should have been finished early in the morning.

The baby calves were herded into a separate pen where they were fed and given fresh water and settled down for a long rest as they were very tired babies.

The men walked their horses to a separate barn where there was fresh hay, grain, and water to greet them.

They also took the saddles, bridles, and blankets from the horse's backs that had carried them on a very hard, long job. They deserved a long rest and their owners always took care of their horses before leaving them in the barn, to feed and rest, before they took care of their own needs.

This is the signature of real 'Gentleman' Cowboys, Ranchers, and Southern Gentlemen. A Southern Code of Ethics and Manners taught through ages of training from one generation to the next.

"The Adventure is over!" said Henry, "Now to tell the boys".

"Oh, my!" said Jerome, "I will leave that little job to you, Mr. Henry".

"Oh no, Sir!" laughed Henry, watching Jerome's frown grow dark.

"I can offer pie to you and the Uncles, but this is a joint effort. Telling the boys and Mother is all our jobs this time," said Henry.

They rode back to Idle Wile' wondering just what Henry had planned for them to tell the boys of the cattle's spoofy whim to get out of the gates and find the corn fields, which, was because the wind was blowing from the west and blew the smell of fresh corn over the pens and barns of the cattle, cows, and calves. "That's a pretty good story," thought Henry, who was trying to decide how to tell the boys that they did not miss an adventure with thieves or Indians or both.

Henry was very glad to let the workers take Justice and Thunder, Jerome's horse, along with Princess and Dakota to the stables for a wash-down, food, and rest with the other horses.

"Uncle Henry! We found some ripe peaches and Sassy made two peach pies for a treat. We have been waiting for you all to come so we could have pie and milk!" shouted the boys, Madeline, and Bella, who were home from a visit with the cousins.

"Aww," said a tired, hungry Henry, who did not want to disappoint the boys, but they had a good story after all. Every one of the farmers was very glad that there wasn't a big problem with Indians, thieves, or pirates.

"Hello boys! That sounds like a great treat! Lead the way to the pie and coffee for us." Smiled Henry and the rest of the men following him into the kitchen where the smell of fresh pies just out of the oven greeted them.

"Hi Ms Bessie, Hi Sassy, I hear you been spoiling some boys while we were gone. Those pies sure smell good, coffee too, great." Smiled Henry. We will just go wash up and be right down for this major treat."

"Yes Sir, Mr. Henry." Said Sassy. "We will go find Ms. Amy and we are ready to serve those pies."

"Thank you, Mam." Said Henry, Jerome, and the Uncles as they all went upstairs to wash up for the treat that was in store for them.

The Pie was delicious.

After the children had their baths they joined the family on the Front Porch.

The Uncles had returned home and Jerome had called it a day riding home after a long tiring day.

Henry took out the little leather pouch from his watch pocket and started making "The Sign of The Cross" to say the Rosary. The children and Amy took up their Rosaries and began the Prayers with Henry.

It had been a long trying day for them all.

Time for Bed.

Good Night Dear Friends.

Josh

Chapter Two

"RUN, CHARLIE, RUN"

Bailey, Ethel M.T.

Charlie woke up to see Lois's smiling face, and she was handing him a fresh cup of coffee. The beautiful bells of the Saint Louis Cathedral Catholic Church in the New Orleans French Quarters were chiming the six o'clock hour in the early morning.

"Good Morning, Mr. Charlie." Said Lois.

"Good Morning Lois, how are you this morning?" Asked a sleepy Charlie.

"I am fine, Mr. Charlie, your Poppa said to tell you that Mass is a little earlier this morning, because it is a Holy Day of Obligation," said Lois.

Charlie sat up in bed and yawned his dreams of the night away, and finished drinking his coffee.

"O.K., Lois, thank you, I had forgotten. Please tell Adam to come in."

"I will, Mr. Charlie; he is right in the hall."

"Thank you Lois." Said Charlie.

Adam came into the room with Charlie's church clothes on his arm. Adam was the Valet for Charlie. He knew what Charlie needed and wanted for each day of the week and the Holidays. He had also packed a small valise for Charlie to take to the country, to visit Henry for a few days.

"Thank you Adam, I think Mama and Poppa are all ready for Mass."

"Yes, Mr. Charlie, they are in the hall." Smiled Adam.

"Well, we better hurry up. They do not like to be just on time. They have to be early, to tell Father Jerome and Father Theriot, 'Good Morning'."

"Yes Sir, I know." Laughed Adam.

"Adam, please bring my valise to the stables, the boys will tie it on the saddle rings on Mooney for me. We are going to the country today, to Henry's place."

"Yes Sir, Mr. Charlie, I'll take it down there on my way to Mass." Adam was a new Catholic and he did not miss daily Mass either.

After Mass, Charlie and his family walked down a little ways to have breakfast at Brennan's Restaurant.

Charlie

After a good meal, Charlie kissed his Mother and took his Father's hand in farewell. His parents were going to their home in the country along the Mississippi River in Plaquemines' Parish, just a few miles south of the city.

Charlie was on his way to get Mooney from the stables. Mooney was ready. The stable boy was waiting for Charlie with Mooney's bridle in hand for Charlie to take.

Charlie threw a silver dollar to the stable boy who grinned and tipped his hat.

Charlie mounted Mooney with the skill of a long knowing relationship with his horse. Mooney gently nudged Charlie's boot to let him know he was a happy horse to have his Master on his back once again.

Mooney was ready to be out of the stables and going riding with Charlie, who always thought his horse knew where they were going and how to get there without any guidance from his Master.

"Oh well" said Charlie to Mooney, "I am happy to let you have your head in most situations and adventures we share. Most times you, Mooney, have more sense than I do." Laughed Charlie, over his own silliness with this horse. Most days Mooney was the only one Charlie had to talk to and Mooney did not talk back. Though he snorted some.

Mooney was company for Charlie on a long ride like today. They were on their way to Henry's Plantation, Idle Wile', a beautiful Mansion with the Bayou Teche' running through the middle in St. Martin's Parish. The famous poet, Longfellow, wrote his beautiful and famous poem, Evangeline, there. The muddy Mississippi River ran on the South side of the home-stead.

"Oh, my mind is really wondering today, Mooney. We need a rest and some dinner, it is already dinner time. Let's go to the little Inn in St. Martinville, a good stable for you and a good meal with friends, for me.

Charlie left Mooney at the stables to be fed and given fresh water. The saddle and blanket came off so he could rest. They were only about half an hour from Henry's home. Not too long a trip now.

Charlie walked into the Inn and picked a table by the window. He was tired and hungry.

As he sat down, his friend and owner of the Inn was crossing the floor with a glass of Red wine and a glass of water, carrying them to Charlie's table.

'What a treat' thought Charlie, as he greeted Buddy V with a big grin.

"Where have you been?" Asked Buddy, as he handed Charlie a food card to choose his meal.

"Gumbo with potatoes, salad, French bread, and bread pudding, looks good to me today." Said Charlie.

"Uh huh" grinned Buddy, "That's what you get every time you stop here. EVERY time." A laughing Buddy said slowly, so Charlie was sure to get the point.

Buddy's servers were busy setting the table for Charlie, but you could hear them snicker on hearing that remark. White napkins, silverware, and a cool pitcher of water was the basic table setting on a sparkling white linen table cloth. Only the best at Buddy's' Place.

Some of Charlie's friends came into the Inn for a meal and they joined Charlie at his table hoping to get the latest gossip of the French Quarters in New Orleans. That was always more interesting than the little town they lived in. Sheriff Jay Cotter took the chair Charlie motioned to him, to join him for Dinner.

"Hello Jay, what have you been up to?" Asked Charlie as he enjoyed his Gumbo. Buddy brought the Sheriff a cool mug of water to cool off with on this hot afternoon.

"Thank you Buddy, It is a really warm for this Fall Season. Oh well, that's weather in Louisiana. Thank God for it, too." Said Jay.

"Well Charlie, I guess you heard about the fact that miserable Pirate, Jean Laffite, is again in these parts with his ships loaded with stolen loot he's plundered from the Spanish, British, and African Merchant ships. We are just waiting for him to throw anchor in his favorite spot, The Bay of St. Helena, about seven miles above Henry's Plantation Idle Wile' and the other farms of the family." Said Jay as he drank the mug of water down.

The Sheriff ordered a dinner of fried Trout and Dressing. 'Yum.' thought Charlie.

"Why he doesn't spread his 'Bad Will' around other shores in Louisiana is beyond me," said a frustrated Sheriff.

"Well, you are way ahead of me where any news is concerned these days. It is pretty calm in the French Quarters but just wait, Mardi Gras Balls and Parades starting in a few days will change all that." Said Charlie.

"We are enjoying the peace and quiet." laughed Charlie.

"Yea, yea, Charlie, we all know how you and Henry are all ready to dance and get all decked out in black tux's and tails to whew and wow the New Orleans' Ladies at the Mardi Gras' Mask Balls. Dining and dancing all night,for several nights, you poor things." Laughed Buddy.

"Uh Huh" grinned Charlie, "especially since you and all our buddies are right there with us to wine and dine the pretty ladies of Louisiana and other states of our U.S. of A., all of whom stream down south at the mention of Mardi Gras'. How you talk my friend. Huh, Jay?!"

"Yep." said Jay, who had more serious problems on his mind just now.

"I suppose we all enjoy the craziness of Mardi Gras, especially since Lent follows on Ash Wednesday, right on the heels of Fat Tuesday. With early morning Mass and Ashes, Fasting, Prayers and Penance, we all seem to be ready for Lent. We get a good rest and cleansing of the rich food and drink we enjoy during the party days. Life is so fair, most times." Finished Charlie with his preaching as Henry would say if he was present.

"Yes, Yes." They all agreed.

The door was slammed hard against the wall as it opened and Ernie Ledet, one of the deputies of the Parish, came in yelling for the Sheriff.

"Sheriff! Charlie! Have you heard the drums of the Biloxi Tribe going crazy as only they know how, on the North shore of the Bayou?" Thomas asked.

"We knew Jean Lafitte was sailing toward the Little Bay of St. Helena. But we didn't know he had landed with his loaded ships of bounty." Said Jay.

"Well, he has and he is already making trouble with his friends the crazy Biloxi Tribe of Indians!" More shouting from Thomas.

"Calm down, calm down, Thomas." said Buddy, handing him a glass of water. 'Now what?' thought Buddy?

Thomas spotted Charlie and he said, "Charlie, I am so glad you are here. I guess you're on your way to Henry's place?"

"Yes I am Thomas, we are going hunting tomorrow, if this problem with Lafitte is not as serious as your news sounds like it is." Answered Charlie, 'Wondering if deer hunting was in their near future at all.'

"I haven't heard any drums today." Said Charlie. "What is the problem with the miserable Indians and Lafitte, now?"

"I just got here and stopped for lunch on the way to Henry's place. What's going on?" Asked Charlie.

"Well, Jean has landed his ships where he thinks he is still safe in the Bay of St. Helena. But we have had that area on watch around the clock since we learned of his special retreat there. We learned this from the Chitimacha Tribe, our friends, the first and last and only time he laid low there." Said Jay.

"I was hoping it would have blown over by now and Lafitte would go to another bayou or swamp this time. I thought the Biloxi Tribe might have heard that we knew of the hiding place of their friend, Lafitte. They have many warriors and maidens that are friends of the Chitimacha. News gets around fast. Maybe not." Finished Jay.

Charlie finished his lunch and sent one of the boys to get Mooney from the stable, while he paid his bill.

Mooney

The Stable boy, Jim, had Mooney all ready for Charlie. Jim caught the silver dollar Charlie tossed to him for taking care of Mooney. Jim looked in his hand and beamed at Charlie for this gift. A dollar! Wow!" Said Jim as he rubbed the coin between his fingers.

Thank you, Mr. Charlie, Gee!" Laughed a happy boy.

Charlie Williams was on the run as fast as he could go on Mooney. Then Mooney threw a shoe in the forest.

Charlie tied Mooney to an old oak tree until he could bring help. Now Charlie would be on foot going to his long time friend's plantation, Idle Wile'. The farm was not too far from where he was leaving Mooney in the forest.

"Quiet, quiet, Mooney." said Charlie, soothing Mooney before he left him. Charlie had swiftly taken off the saddle and blanket and laid it beside the old tree that had many roots growing above ground to catch the rain drops before the ground gulped them all up.

Charlie stooped down to re-tie his shoe strings to tighten them for the run he'd have to make to the Plantation, faster, safer, and easier. Charlie was not used to running at break-neck speed anymore, unless he had Mooney under him doing all the work. He loosened his tie, all ready, set, and GO! Charlie went south from where Mooney was left. He knew the direction he needed to go to get help.

He was running hard and jumping over tree roots and brush as fast as he could and still keep his balance for the next steps ahead.

Then he heard the drums, beating, beating, their warning of war coming to the white man's country and homes.

Out of breath and sweating, he was running for help and safety. Suddenly, Charlie caught sight of Henry's big white Plantation home. The porch lanterns were lit and downstairs the lamps and candles were glowing with warmth into the dark Charlie was running from. The Living Room, Library, and Dining Room were lit with candles and lanterns too. Charlie could see the fireplace logs burning brightly, welcoming all who came this way.

The big lanterns were like beacons in the dark sky surrounding Charlie. The barn was aglow with dark figures carrying big lanterns to light their way. They were tending the animals at the end of a long work day. The cows had to be milked for the second and last time of the day. Animals had to be fed and water put in their water troves and quieted down for the night ahead.

Lantern

Charlie took the last few steps onto the big front porch.

He shouted as loud as he could for his good friend and co-conspirator of all great and small adventures they shared, Henry.

"HENRY! HENRY!" yelled Charlie with all his breath and might that he had left in his aching body from running hard through the forest.

The big doors flew open. "What wrong wit you Mon," shouted el Rico, 'The Butler of all the needs of the Arrington Family was from India.'

"Mon, Mr. Charlie, you come into this house. You look like a ghost from the dead, Sir".

Then el Rico heard the drums with their static beat of the tom tom drummers, which could only mean trouble. el Rico turned red in fear of what this could mean.

"Take my arm, Mr. Charlie, don't fall down Mon," he cautioned. "I help you,

Mr. Charlie," said el Rico.

A large shadow filled the doorway.

"Oh, Mr. Henry," said el Rico, as Henry flew down the steps to help el Rico with his friend, Charlie.

"What has happened to you, Charlie? Oh my Lord, the tom toms are beating a warning tonight. What is happening? What is going on?" A very puzzled Henry asked his friend.

"Where did you leave Mooney? Never mind for now Charlie, let's get you inside. Here we are, a few more steps to the fireplace." Henry, and el Rico, with Charlie in the middle, fell into the big hall of the mansion.

"Oh, moi Bon Dieu (My Good Lord)," whispered Amy.

"Henry bring him in here, by the fire, he is white as a sheet." Amy had big tears falling down her cheeks.

"What could have happened to him." she moaned.

"el Rico, please bring him a glass of water and a glass of red wine, Dépêche' Toie' (Hurry up)!" el Rico."

Henry was worried to see his friend in shock.

"What has happened to you, Charlie? Oh my Lord, the tom toms are restless tonight. What is going on?" a very puzzled Henry asked his friend.

"And where did you leave Mooney?"

'I wonder what could have happened to Charlie. Why are the drums of the Biloxi Tribe beating a warning to white people and the Chitimacha Tribe? Why?' questioned Henry to himself.

While Henry knew Charlie was here this evening to go hunting in the morning, he debated on where he left Moonie and why. 'Well,' decided Henry, 'I'll give him some time to catch his breath and have a glass of wine, to recuperate. That should work.' thought Henry, as he watched Charlie cool down.

Charlie was getting all of el Rico's attention while Amy's attention drifted to the subject of the French Language she and her family spoke so well. They had been educated in Northern France before coming to this country.

The Ursuline Nun's taught school in their Convent, located in New Orleans, to all the children of the city and surrounding Parish's and Plantations. Most of the Nuns were from France. They taught Parisian French.

'How the times were changing,' thought Amy.

Thank God for Idle Wild, the Arrington farm, and the surrounding farms of her family. There were five family plantations. In all over four-hundred-thousand Arpan's (acres) of land for each farm. A lot of the land was still in forest acres. The French word, Arpan, is the French measurement of acres of land in Louisiana. None of the children escaped the teachings of the Nuns and the Priests of New Orleans, and they were much better off because of it.

Our beautiful Louisiana was named for the King and Queen of France, Louis, and Anna.

Our State has been owned by different Countries and has had Ten Foreign flags flying over the state at different times in its early history. The last one is The United States of America. Louisiana is our History And Heritage.

'Oh well, I am drifting away from my poor Charlie.' Thought Amy.

Charlie was sitting on a big chair. Henry was sitting on the sofa.

el Rico was holding a silver tray of tinted wine glasses of red wine and a crystal pitcher of cool water, with water glasses on the side table and a bowl of fresh baked crackers.

"Whew!" Said Charlie, letting out a long held breath of air.

"Henry, get the men and horses ready for a fight. This warning came from the Sheriff in town."

Said Charlie.

"What, What!" Yelled Henry at Charlie. "What happened? I heard the drums of the Biloxi Tribe, those crazy Indians know better than to threaten the white people and the Chitimacha Tribe, who are our friends and will fight with us. What stirred them up?"

Meanwhile, the well-known Louisiana Pirate Jean Lafitte had silently slid his ships into the little Bay of St. Helena on the northern side of the bayou. The Pirates were only five or six miles upstream from the Arrington Plantations.

Henry sent for Jerome and asked him to have the five family Plantations patrolled by the workers, with their rifles and pistols loaded, in case of trouble, and to send a message to the Uncles of what was happening.

The Biloxi Tribe's drums stopped abruptly.

Henry and Charlie went out on the front porch to see if they could see anything around the property.

All was quiet. Then out of the night a Chitimacha' Warriors' yell, at the edge of the lawn of Idle Wile', could be heard.

"Lil' Wolf." Whispered Henry.

The Sheriff and Lil' Wolf came riding up to the porch where Charlie and Henry were standing.

"Hello Sheriff and Lil' Wolf. My friends, how did you know of the danger to the Plantations, tonight?"

"Charlie just arrived a few minutes ago and warned us of the danger and then the Biloxi Tribe drummers were beating the tom toms wildly for a few minutes. What's going on?" Asked Henry.

"Well Henry, we got the news of trouble brewing this way at the same time as Charlie did. After Charlie left the restaurant in St. Martinville, we decided you might need help from the Sheriff, the Deputies and Lil' Wolf, and the Chitimacha Tribe." Explained the Sheriff.

"So we met in the woods at the edge of Idle Wile' and attacked the Biloxi Tribe as they were creeping up on Idle Wile'. We routed them out for good. We will patrol the Plantations for a couple of nights to make sure they won't return." Said the Sheriff.

"Thank you Sheriff and Lil' Wolf, your help is very much appreciated. I will get Ms Bessie and Sassy to make up some sandwiches and coffee for you and your men." Said Henry.

"Thank you Henry. We will be here till day-break and again tomorrow night. We'll say good night to your family and workers." Said Jay, Lil' Wolf bowed his head in agreement.

Henry and Charlie waved good-bye to the men surrounding the Plantations to provide protection during the night.

Henry and Charlie went inside to the welcoming fire-place and told Amy of the danger that was diverted by the Sheriff and Lil' Wolf, and of the Sentries that would keep watch over their homes during the night.

There were no more incidents from the Biloxi Tribe for some time to come.

Charlie, Henry, and Amy had a glass of sherry and said another decade of the Rosary to thank God for the help of friends and this peaceful evening in their homes.

Bine Siad mes' Ami. Good Night, my Friends.

Chapter Three

"EXPLOSION"

Bailey, Ethel M.T.

Everyone was sleeping soundly at the Idle Wile' farm, it was Tuesday, four o'clock in the morning. Very early.

There was a soft knock on the front door, then quiet.

A stronger fist struck the door a second strike with knuckles applied.

"Moo, Moo." said the cows. The knocking on the big front door was waking up the animals earlier than usual; they usually woke up with the dawn. So did the people who served the coffee in bed. Yes, every one of the family got coffee in bed, even the children.

Amy was quicker than Henry putting on her robe and slippers. The robe was on the end of the bed, her slippers were on the floor. She grabbed the pistol that rested on the night stand that was on Amy's sleeping side of her bed. And, yes, it is always loaded. The door to her bedroom was locked during the day.

Amy was going downstairs when Henry caught up with her and asked her to let him go first to answer the door. Amy was in agreement. It was one thing to be without a man in the house to answer the door at night, however, there was always a man in this house at night. The butler lived there and Jerome, who was a bachelor, would sleep there whenever Henry was away.

"I'm coming, I'm coming," said Henry to the person on the other side of the big doors. He unlocked the door and opened it slowly. You never knew who would be on the other side of the door, at night especially.

"Oh my Good Lord," whispered Henry to the half–naked and beaten bloody man in front of him.

There was blood and bruises all over him. So much so, Henry did not recognize him.

"Mama, please don't come any further. Call Ms Bessie to wake up el Rico to come and help me. He has lots of injuries. We need lots of help. Please send Sassy for Jerome and the Uncles."

The man at the door almost fell on Henry as he came close to him in order to help him inside the Great Hall.

el Rico came into the hall with a glass of water and a warm wet towel. Amy had told him of the problem with this early morning disturbance.

el Rico ran to Henry to help him with the broken man at the door

"el Rico, please help me take him to the bottom step of the stairs where I can help him and see how hurt he is."

Amy went into the kitchen to get a tray of coffee, prepared by Sassy, for Henry and his helpers to fortify them for the job ahead.

"Oh my Good Lord," whispered Henry to the half–naked and beaten, bloody man in front of him.

Henry took the towel from el Rico and told the man that he would clean his wounds as easy as he could. Then he would be able to see how badly and where he was hurt. The man seemed to trust Henry and waved his good hand in agreement.

Henry could not help shaking his head in astonishment at the hateful damage done to this man as he washed his face, arms, and hands.

Henry concentrated on the bloody flesh he was softly cleaning in order to treat him and make him more comfortable and give him medicine to relieve the pain.

As Henry concentrated on cleaning the wounds of the injured man, el Rico was watching the face of the man.

el Rico gave a big 'Gasp' as he recognized the man in front of him.

Henry looked at el Rico, startled by his reaction.

Henry looked closely at the stranger and shook his head, strongly, not believing his eyes.

As he looked at el Rico who was shaking his head to affirm the identity of the man in front of them. The man was a good friend of theirs and their families.

The Sheriff of St Mary's Parish, Jay Cotter, was the bruised and beaten man in front of them!

"Sheriff, what in the world happened to you?" Asked Henry watching his friend trying to adjust to the safety he found with his friend, Henry.

"You got a bit of whiskey," asked Jay, trying to see Henry out of his swollen, red eyes.

"I understand the need for your choice of drink, Jay, but those lips tell me you better have a little gram of Sherry." Said Henry looking at el Rico to help him with the request for a glass of Sherry.

"Yes." Slurred the painful lips of the Sheriff.

"What happened?" Whispered Amy to Henry.

"We don't know yet Mama, he needs a little more time. He is really hurt." replied Henry.

"I am much better and I never thought I would be safe again. Then I ran-upon Idle Wile' just as I thought I was lost in my misery, forever. Man, I should have gotten the deputies to come with me, but I thought I knew what I was getting into. But no, not a chance could I have ever thought of what was really happening in the Village of Bay St. Lewis.

Thank you el Rico, this sherry really is good." Smiled Jay, as he frowned because his cracked lips were painful to smile, talk, or drink sherry for that matter.

Jay, you think you can walk into the Library, if we help you?" Asked Henry as he motioned to el Rico to take Jay's' left arm under his shoulder where he was not hurt too much. Henry took Jay's' right arm to lift him off the steps to take a few steps into Library, the room Henry needed him to go to check him over.

"Uhhh.", grunted Jay, not wanting to move. He knew Henry wanted to examine his wounds in order to give him some medical attention. That knowledge did not help the pain.

Henry steered Jay and el Rico to the couch where Jay would be comfortable. Amy and Ms Bessie had gone into the linen closet to gather sheets, pillows, and blankets to make a bed on the couch for Jay.

Sassy was in the kitchen making mash potatoes, heating milk, and making custard for the injured Sheriff, and the family, of course. All of the kitchen help were washing dishes, cleaning up and asking the same question.

"Just what could have happened to the Sheriff of the Town who had lots of strong men to follow his lead and help him and keep everyone from harm?" Everyone was disturbed by this tragedy that happened to the sheriff. Just what is it?

Henry cleaned and used cat gut from the insides of animals after it was washed, dried and twisted into thread and wound on a wooden spool that he whittled and carved for that purpose. This thread would be used to stitch up Jay's wounds which was too many to count. el Rico was using clean towels to keep up with the bleeding. Amy went into the kitchen to get a cup of coffee and Sassy brought a tray of hot cups of coffee into the Library for the three men.

I.J., Bud, Jimmy, and Jerome came into the library with Ms Bessie, helping her with glasses of water and crystal goblets of red wine for all.

"Oh my goodness, Jay," exclaimed I. J., "Did you run into a Black Bear from the Islands?"

"Uncle, we haven't gotten to that part, yet. We're too busy cleaning wounds and trying to stop the excessive bleeding, before we lose our patient. OH, OH, what have we here?" exclaimed Henry, finding another injury that needed his immediate attention.

"Oh, no, Doc I don't need you to keep poking me and sewing me up, not to mention el Rico rubbing my skin off. Oh, so sorry fellows, I am just hurt, sore, and tired. I am so banged up, I never felt like this before in my life." said Jay.

"Well Jay, I have some good news, and I have a little bad news." Henry chided his good friend. "But, before we go into that, let's have our wine and Sassy's treats she made for you and the rest of her family too. Yum." Teased Henry.

Everyone was served by Sassy and el Rico who then returned to the kitchen to get a tray of fresh coffee. They returned to the Library to the cheers of the men.

Henry had sent his Mother, Amy, back up to bed; she was looking tired and worried. He gave instructions to Ms Bessie to make Amy a little sweet cup of hot spearmint tea to help her rest.

As the men were gathered around the fire place and the couch the sheriff was lying on, I.J. asked Henry to give Jay, a large dose of Ether because he knew what type of surgery Henry had to perform on him.

"Yes, Uncle, el Rico is mixing up a portion, now." Agreed Henry.

"Wait! Wait a minute Doc! More surgery on what? May I ask?" Said a miserable Jay.

"Jay, I am so sorry but you have a broken knee cap. After we finish eating, I am going to let el Rico and Uncle I.J. give you a portion of Ether to keep the pain away. You will be asleep. Don't worry; both el Rico and Uncle I.J. are experts in giving antiseptic medicine. I will be close by to watch in case I'm needed. Do you feel able, before the Ether takes full effect, to tell us a little of what happened to you out in woods?"

Yes, I want to tell you, I hardly believe it myself." Jay said, as he started thinking of just what he had been through yesterday and earlier last night.

"I was behind the jail, watering the horses and trimming their hooves, when three of the men who were sent to jail by Judge McBride just yesterday started talking in whispers in their cell, but in a little while, they got louder and louder. The one named Carl Edgecombe started yelling at the other two.

Something about the cash they were going to split when the barrels of whiskey were ready to be bottled, for sale to the Americans and Mexicans. It was over three-hundred barrels of "White Lighting." said the Sheriff. "That's about three-thousand, eight-ounce bottles of whiskey, at 108 Proof. That can kill a man or make him go crazy. That amount is selling at about five-dollars a bottle. I can't even add that high." said the Sheriff.

"Me neither," said I.J., the Professor of the Parish.

"I went talk to the Judge and told him what I had heard the men talking about." continued Jay. "The judge asked me what I had in mind concerning the men and the illegal brew of whiskey in the woods. I had this idea that the judge could give them a pardon for twenty-four hours. I think they will leave town and join their friends at the stills in the woods where all that whiskey is just waiting to be bottled up. I want to follow them and get the location of those stills so we can bust them down before they get more illegal help, from the Biloxi Tribe and other criminals from New Orleans. That Whiskey is valuable and illegal."

Jay took a breath of air and a sip of sherry before he could continue his adventure into the White Lightning Market, "The thing is, the Feds will get wind of this valuable cargo to be found here in Louisiana and they will 'jump' on it and they won't wait for a warrant or checking with the State and Local Law Enforcement Offices of Louisiana. The Feds will not provide Louisiana Law Enforcement Agencies with a time table, or pertinent information and plans they will make in their own organization, without informing us. Without even, 'Your State, Your Call" protocol. Not a 'Fare -do–well' for cooperation or sharing the Federal Funds with Louisiana for destroying such a big illegal operation."

"You are so right Jay, I know it's got to be frustrating." Agreed Henry considering Jay's rant concerning his job and commitment to the Sheriff's Office, not to mention The State of Louisiana's' Legal Rights.

"Well, we all know the 'Damn Yankees' have no manners what so ever." Declared Bud.

'The War between the North and the South is starting all over again' Smiled Henry to himself.

"Look Jay, we want to hear the rest of this problem you ran into yesterday, but you are getting very weak and we need to get on with the knee surgery before you are too weak to be able to stand the pressure surgery brings." A worried Henry said.

"Aww," said Bud and Jimmy. "No, no, we don't mean that, Jay! Henry is right. The most important thing right now is your health."

I.J. had drawn a map of the area Jay was talking about where the 'White Lighting Stills', were located in the woods and brewing gallons of illegal whiskey.

"Jay, I will ask Jerome and Uncle Jimmie to run into town and tell the Judge what you have told us so far and the condition you're in on your return home, or at least, to my home." Said Henry.

'Uncle I.J., please send that map you drew up of the location of the stills to Judge McBride as well. He will know just what to do with it." Said Henry, as he signaled el Rico to put a white sheet on the Library table and go get the folded towels to accept the Ether needed to put Jay into a deep sleep for the length of the surgery.

Henry was speaking softly to Jay to help calm him down for the surgery.

"Jay, do you understand just what we will do in the surgery?" Asked Henry, as he directed el Rico to put a few drops of Ether on the clean-folded towel and be ready to cover the sheriff's face with it slowly as possible as not to hurt his injuries. Henry nodded his head and el Rico lowered the towel closer to Jay's nose from above his head.

"Yes Henry, I do understand. I will I be here tonight after the surgery?" Asked Jay, while keeping an eye on el Rico's progress with the towel that smelled to him like, 'a kind relief from his pain.'

"Yes, Jay, you will be here with us tonight and many nights to come." answered Henry as he lowered el Rico's hand to cover the lower half of Jay's face with the towel for a few seconds.

"UMMMMMM," replied Jay, trying to say 'No Way' to Henry's verdict concerning where he would be after the surgery. He would be at Idle Wile' for an eternity, he guessed. Then he was asleep.

Up came the towel from Jay's face, while Henry checked to see if Jay needed a little more Ether before he could proceed. Henry waited a few minutes for the Ether to take affect before he could proceed to patch Jay's many wounds without causing him any pain. In fact, relief from all the pain Jay had been in was one of the main reasons Henry chose to use the Ether.

Henry took his hand from el Rico's while Jay was given a little more Ether; el Rico performed his job, just as Henry had taught him many years ago.

Henry and el Rico listened for the deep and steady breathing they wanted to hear from Jay's relaxed body in order to start the surgery that would mend and sooth Jay's broken body and mind.

The three men watched the Sheriff's body slowly relax and his breading slowly became a deep and healing rhythm.

Henry, I.J., and el Rico proceeded with all the different areas of Jay's body that needed mending.

The knee was the most serious of the needed surgery. That was the area Henry began the process of the making Jay whole again.

The other repairs of Jay's body followed as Henry and the other men moved along each damaged area until Jay was a mass of stitches and bandages. In all, this surgery took a couple of hours until all of the wounds were repaired.

The sheriff would have a long recovery time. Henry was not ready to address the question of how to tell Jay at this time. He, I.J., and el Rico were very tired, hungry, and just plain beat.

Ms Bessie came into the room slowly from the Library door where she and Sassy had been keeping watch over Henry and his team who were working so hard.

Henry saw Ms Bessie and Sassy, followed by four or five other workers, come into the room that was in tatters from the process of a surgery taking place here.

Henry nodded to Ms Bessie and the other people following her into the room. Ms Bessie could read Henry's mind and knew just what was needed now that the work of the Doctor and his Assistants was complete.

Henry, I.J, and el Rico began the delicate job of moving Jay from the Library table to the bed in the bedroom next to the Library. Amy and Ms Bessie had made that room ready for Jay while the Ether was taking its effect on Jay's senses, nerves, and pain.

The servants began picking up Ether towels, dirty sheets, and all kinds of implements and tools used in the surgery. While the men picked up the linen and dirty towels that were on the floor in the process of the surgery.

Henry crossed the Library to thank Ms Bessie and her team for their much needed help in the process of cleaning up the mess in the Library. All done without any instructions from Henry or Amy, as always was the way of the good people of the Plantations of the Arrington's.

I.J. and el Rico told Henry, 'Good Morning', as they went their separate ways to get a much needed bath, food, and rest.

"A job well done." Were Henry's last words to his helpers as he started up the great stairs from which he had descended last night, as his nights' rest was interrupted.

The day was well on its way; it was almost lunch time as Henry was getting dressed. As he finished a much needed bath he had sent el Rico, who usually waited on Henry hand and foot, to his room next to Henry's to take care of himself after their mutual ordeal of a big surgery.

Henry and el Rico left Jay with Sassy and Jeromy, and went to the kitchen to have dinner and coffee. Then they went to their bedrooms to have a bath, clean clothes, and a nap.

Henry woke up and wanted a hot cup of coffee on the front porch while rocking in his favorite rocker in the cool breeze. After he checked on Jay who was sound asleep and so was Sassy, she had a long hard day, and Jay had a good color and no fever to speak of. Henry carefully put a pillow under Sassy's head, and tip-toed out of the room.

El Rico had just opened Henry's door when the house rocked on its giant pillars with a gigantic BOOM! BOOM! BOOM! That blasted the morning quiet of the Plantations.

"What was that?!" Asked Henry, looking at el Rico, who was as white as a sheet.

"I am SO SURE, I don't know!" Answered el Rico, in his fear and shock.

Henry jumped over the chair that was in his way and reached the door just as Amy opened it to go into his room.

Henry almost fell over Amy. He grabbed the edge of the door that helped him catch his balance.

"B O O M! B O O M! B O O M!" Said the Angry Air, surrounding the Plantations' fields.

The cattle, horses, and chickens went clucking and cock-A-doodling for all they were worth and running crazy all over the yard.

The men working in the cane fields and orange groves, gardens and dairy barns, came running as fast as they could back to the house seeking word of what the 'Big Booms' were all about.

They were worried about just how much danger they and their families were in.

Henry came into the yard to meet his family, workers, and friends.

"Please, do not be worried or afraid of the explosions in the woods. It is our friends, the Judge, Sheriff Deputies and Uncles, Lil' Wolf and his Tribe, taking care of the illegal stills of whiskey in the woods. I'll bet my bottom dollar that Lil' Wolf and his warriors used their flaming arrows to destroy the Devil's Whiskey Stills."

Indian with bow

"Good riddance to bad rubbish, I say," said Henry, with Amy's Blessing.

Henry came out of the Library after checking on Jay and his sitter. He was headed toward the kitchen as Ms Bessie was taking a tray of coffee and sandwiches to the porch where Amy was resting.

Henry made a right hand turn to the front door of the Mansion and stepped onto the porch just as he caught sight of a cream-colored Palomino horse known to everyone in the Parish as, 'Cloud 1', the Judge's horse.

Uncle Jimmie and Jerome's horses were galloping along each side of the Judge's horse. The Uncles and the Judge were safe at home.

"Now, isn't that Justice to see those three high tailing it right to me?" laughed Henry.

"After all, that was the plan!" Said Henry, shaking his head.

Henry waved to the horsemen headed his way, at the end of their mission, as they galloped toward Idle Wile'.

Meanwhile, the Louisiana Lawmen, Deputies, and Marshals headed toward town to protect their families and the citizens of the town. The Chitimacha Chief, Lone Eagle, and his Warriors were back to the Chitimacha Village in Charenton, Louisiana, following their partnership with the Judge, the Deputies, and the Louisiana State Marshals. Not to mention Henry's Uncles. They were all in the fight against the Whiskey Barons and the whiskey brew known as 'Moon Shine,' and 'White Lightening' stills found in the great woods.

The men were dirty, dead tired, hungry, and worried of the repercussions of any friends of the White Lighting Whiskey Barons. If there were any left, that is, after the fight that took place in the woods.

Henry sent one of the children playing in the yard to tell Ms Bessie to expect company in just a few minutes.

Amy came out onto the porch from the hall of the house when she heard the message Henry sent to Ms Bessie.

The three men rode up to the porch and dismounted with huge grunts of tiredness, hunger, dust and dirt covering them.

Any went into the house to find some clean clothes from her husband's closet for the Judge until they could send for his own from town.

Amy then joined the men on the porch and took the Judge inside to show him to a guest bedroom and bath.

He thanked Amy for her kindness by kissing her hand. Henry sent up a glass of wine and a few biscuits to the Judge's bedroom by Sassy, whose hand the Judge kissed also. Sassy giggled all the way down the stairs; she couldn't wait to tell Ms Bessie! That's the first time anyone ever kissed her hand, she told Ms Bessie and Ms Amy as they both smiled at her delight.

Uncle Jimmy and Jerome went to the back door for a glass of water and a glass of wine before going to hit the big brown barrels in the barn where they often bathed when they were so dirty, tired, and stinky. There was lots of clean water, fluffy towels, and lots of soap. Old pants, shirts in all sizes were clean and on the barn shelves ready for use.

The Judge came out to the porch after a sound, short nap and thanked Amy for the clothes left on the bed from her late husband's closet. He was ready for dinner; he carried his empty wine glass in his left hand hoping for a refill. It had been a long hard day. Not on the 'Bench, Judging' day, but on horseback riding '60 to nothin' out of Town', day.

He was so right. Amy had the bottle of wine and her own petite wine goblet. The Judge toasted Amy and sipped his wine while swinging in his favorite seat, on his favorite porch, with favorite friends.

The children came out on the porch in their white gowns, all bathed, fed, and teeth brushed, carrying their little Rosaries.

Henry and Amy took out their Rosaries. The Judge took his out of his watch pocket.

"In the Name of The Father," the Judge started the Rosary. He had much to be thankful for, as well as the rest of the family.

Good Night, Dear Friends.

Chapter Four

"LIL' WOLF"

Bailey, Ethel M.T.

Sassy and el Rico were in the kitchen sipping the first cup of coffee of the Day!

A tray was set with fancy china cups, sugar bowl, and cream pitcher all ready for Ms Bessie to pour the hot-mellow coffee of the New Orleans French Market Coffee Shop Beans, purchased in bags for the family, friends, and workers to enjoy during the day.

Sugar was made on the Plantation from the sweet sugar cane crop grown on the farms. The cane was boiled in the big hot kettles at Harvest time; the hot fire renders the juice of the sugar cane into grains of sugar.

The gentle dairy cows give a thick rich, sweet cream that rises to the top of the milk after the milk is scalded, cooled, and put in clean milk bottles to bring to the ice cellar to keep until the five Arrington families and town markets pick up the supplies for home use and sales.

The dairy cows are milked twice a day which gives a great supply of milk each day for use and sale. The merchants of the grocery stores and restaurants in St.Martinville are happy to have all this work performed for the customers they serve. This is a cash source of money used by the farms to purchase material for clothes and other necessary needs for life in general not grown on the farm.

St. Martinville was named after St. Martin de Pours, Priest of the Holy Catholic Church, founded in the town of St. Martinville. He came from France.

While on the farm, it was very early in the morning. el Rico and Sassy were making the rounds of serving coffee to the family 'in bed', each member in turn. This was a French tradition carried on for many years in France, maybe other countries too.

It is interesting to learn that the coffee bean is roasted over an open fire in the yard of the farm until it is brown and roasted to perfection. The coffee beans are then cooled and ground in a coffee grinder that is nailed or bolted to a post on the back porch. Handy to use when needed. You could hear the grinder for acres around early in the morning doing its job for families and friends alike. Coffee was served to workers and visitors during the day, to sip, visit, and enjoy the company of family and friends. It was another blessing from Our Lord, Jesus.

It's early on Idle Wile' this morning and there will be some disappointed boys today. No fishing trip in this down pour: thunder and lightning early, early in the morning. Mama was waking up slowly; she got out of bed. She opened a drawer in the chest and took out a blessed piece of palm to burn in a little bowl and made the sign of the cross. She kneeled by her bed and said a prayer for God to stop the bad weather from causing any damage to the farms and families living in the area.

In a few minutes of prayers, the thunder and lightning moved on.

It was almost daylight as Amy put on her robe and went downstairs to the kitchen to make a fresh pot of coffee. It was no surprise to her that she could smell the coffee brewing on the pot-belly stove. Ms Bessie was up and knitting a red winter scarf for Sassy, who was cold natured, while she had a little time.

Amy and Ms Bessie had the first coffee of the day as they talked of the family and friends they would see and the chores they were to do.

The sun is rising in the East, gently getting brighter and warmer as it moved over the land and the farms. The trees were sprinkled with dew. The sun danced over the roses and daisies as well. It was slowly rising over the water and the green grass. The rain had moved on leaving a beautiful warm day.

Ms Bessie and Sassy were going to each bedroom with a tray of coffee-filled cups for the waking of the family and friends of the family. Jay was getting better by the day. He was treated to a fresh cup of coffee in the morning, as well.

The family was gathered in the kitchen for breakfast. Ms Bessie was making biscuits and pancakes, the family's favorite. They each liked butter and syrup with these early morning treats. Sassy poured several glasses of cold milk and a few cups of fresh coffee for the adults.

Henry and el Rico were in Jay's bedroom, checking on his wounds. They were healing faster than Henry or Jay thought possible. He would soon be back in town, taking care of the law breakers once again. The Judge visited every afternoon to keep Jay informed on the progress of the Marshalls and Deputies cleaning up the rest of the criminals involved in the illegal whiskey- brewing stills in the forest.

The Marshal's hired the men in town to clean up the mess left by the explosion of the whiskey stills. The men were glad to get the work and the Judge was happy to use the Federal Funds to pay for the cleanup. All's well that ends well.

In the kitchen, the family were standing behind their chairs waiting for Henry and Jerome to come to breakfast.

el Rico was setting up a chair with pillows and blankets to move Jay from the bed to the chair for a much needed rest from lying on his back constantly for so many days.

Henry helped el Rico move Jay to the chair. "Oh, Happy Day,' He sang to celebrate Jay's big move to a chair after all he had been through.

Jay's remark was "It feels good, just to walk a few steps and get out of bed."

"Yes," said Henry, "I thought so. Sassy has your breakfast on a tray. I'm going to get my meal too." Said a hungry Henry as he left the room saying to Jay, "I'll see you later, Jay".

A friend of Henry's came to Idle Wile' to relieve el Rico of nursing Jay for a few days so el Rico could rest and go fishing with Henry and the boys, who were patiently waiting for that day. Marshal, a friend of Henry's, came into the kitchen from the back porch.

"Good Morning Marshal!" greeted Amy and the boys.

"Henry told us you would be here today. Have you eaten breakfast?" Asked Amy.

"Yes Mam, Mr. Henry told me I was sitting with Mr. Jay, today," said Marshal.

"Yes," said Amy, "Sassy will take you through! Please carry that tray for Sassy and follow her to Jay's bedroom. Thank you, Marshal."

"Let us know if you need anything." Added Ms Bessie.

"el Rico will relieve you, Marshal, for breaks." Said Amy.

Sassy went into the hall carrying a pitcher of milk. Marshal followed behind with the tray of food for Jay and el Rico.

Sassy would help Jay with his fork, knife, cup, and glass; his fingers were still hurting from the horrible night in the woods.

Henry waited by the open door for Sassy and Marshal to enter. el Rico was helping Jay settle in the chair by the little table. A candle sat on the table to light the table setting for Jay's first meal out of bed in three days.

"Three damn days!" Jay would tell you. "Nothing wrong with his patience!!!" Henry noticed.

el Rico shook his head in agreement.

All of a sudden, in the quiet of the morning, the family sitting at the table enjoying their breakfast heard a noise coming from the edge of the woods across the lawn.

"Woooo! Woooo! Yeeee!" yelled Lil' Wolf at the top of his lungs. Henry knew that yell well. The slow mournful whooping sound of the wolf came again. Henry, finished his coffee in one gulp, excused himself and the boys to Amy, gently pushed his and the boy's chairs back under the table AND picked up the two boys, one under each arm, and ran to the back porch all the way to the screen door. He jumped down the steps and landed the boys on their feet beside him.

Amy and Ms Bessie were not far behind them. This is an occasion in their life when this beautiful, wild, perfectly mannered young Indian boy came to call.

Lil' Wolf

Lil Wolf walked out of the Forest, between two beautiful Indian Ponies, Paints, to be exact.

Another long 'W h o aww,' followed just to make sure the family knew just who was coming out from the woods.

Henry waved and yelled back, "Welcome my friend, Lil Wolf." and on the side he asked Amy to send el Rico to get the Judge and the Uncles, pronto! "Yes, Yes", agreed Amy, as she ran to the door.

Lil' Wolf started running in the middle of the two horses. He hung onto the ropes tied around their necks and as he ran, faster and faster, he leapt onto the backs of each pony, his legs wide apart. He hit the ground between the horses with one jump and was back on their backs, facing backwards.

"Wow, Wow," said the boys, and by this time the Uncles had arrived just in time to catch this wonderful treat.

"How does he do THAT?" Asked Bud to the air.

Henry, who had seen this trick many times in the Chitimacha' Village, Smiled and said nothing.

"Lil' Wolf, my friend. What a wonderful treat you have given us this morning. You are so welcomed here. To what do we owe this visit? "Asked Henry with a huge smile and a hug for Lil' Wolf.

The boys, and now the cousins who had arrived, were spelled bound. "What a treat, why don't we see more of him?" Josh wondered out loud, nudging Noah, to ask Uncle Henry this question. "Uhhh no," replied a stupefied Noah.

"Well, Lil' Wolf, come inside and greet an old friend of yours who will be so glad to see you. He and el Rico were watching your ride from a window in the downstairs bedroom." Said Henry, as he steered the whole party into the house through the front door.

"Jay has had a tremendous accident in the forest a couple of nights ago, Lil' Wolf." Said Henry to his friend.

"I know, my friend." Whispered Lil' Wolf to Henry. Henry's eyes flamed with interest and observation of his good friend. Wondering just what Lil' Wolf knew of Jay's terrible night at the whiskey stills in the forest.

They entered the hall and all followed Henry and Lil' Wolf to the bedroom off the Library where Jay, el Rico, and Marshal were patiently waiting the arrival of the guest. Well, as usual, Jay was not very patient, but we understand.

Sassy and Ms Bessie came into the hall with a tray of coffee, cream, and sugar. And a tray of glasses and a pitcher of Root Beer for the children and Lil' Wolf. He loved the white man's treats. Two of the kitchen maids were making sandwiches and little bowls of vegetable soup for a petit brunch for everyone. Food, as always, is on the scene, too.

Lil' Wolf thanked Sassy with a low bow and a smile for his cup of coffee, " sweeter than sweet", said Sassy, as she placed his glass of Root Beer next to his chair on a petit tab, little table. She knew he could reach it easy there. He is always a very special guest to the family and friends alike.

Henry, always watching Lil' Wolf, smiled and thought, 'This is why I love this little boy, ever since he has been born to the beautiful "Moon Flower!'

She named him Lil' Wolf because the 'She Wolves cried all night' – the night he was born. They wailed, is what Moon Flower said. "I don't know why" – she added later on.

Lil' Wolf was a 'friend and a foe' of the big wolf pack that roamed the forest.

Henry addressed the men in the bedroom, "Jay we are about to have a great friend of mine to come to see you!" He smiled.

"Lil' Wolfs a great friend of mine." Said Jay, through battered lips that still hurt a lot.

Meanwhile, the Judge walked into Jay's bedroom carrying a cup of coffee given to him at the door by Ms Bessie.

"Welcome, Gentlemen." Greeted Henry, shaking hands all around. Lil Wolf and el Rico put forward their hands with a smile for Henry, too. Then Jay – put his good hand out too ---All were laughing when Amy walked in and said, "What a joyful group! "I'll tell you later." promised Henry.

The men bowed to Amy and she gave a kiss to all and especially Lil' Wolf and Jay.

The whole room of company smiled at Amy as she took a chair by Henry – not to miss a thing!

I.J., called the boys, Josh, Noah, Ben, the girls, Maddie and Bella, and the cousins, to hear the story. They sat on the floor!

"Jay, when you are ready, start at the beginning of your miss—adventure," Henry said.

"Henry, if you don't mind, I would like to start and save Jay the part that begins with me." Said the Judge.

"Good idea, Judge McBride," agreed Henry. "Anything to save Jay a little pain."

"Well, last Tuesday, Jay was behind the jail taking care of the horses when he heard this conversation between three men in jail for breaking the peace while drunk in St. Martinville." Started the Judge to tell his part of Jay's story and awful condition.

"Jay told me they were having a conversation about 'illegal whiskey stills' they had deep in the woods. They were making 'White Lighting'. It is made in alcohol strength of 108 Proof that equals poison. It's against the Law in the States of Louisiana, Arkansas, and Alabama. Runs men crazy! It's called 'Rot Gut' in most households in this country. It is very dangerous." Said the Judge.

"They were talking about hundreds of barrel, of whiskey ready to bottle into thousands of quart bottles. Crazy rich stuff, big money." Said the Judge.

"Jay came to me with this ideal of turning them loose Tuesday afternoon so he could track them to the stills – there are no trails in 'Le Gran Chenier" – "The Big Woods," finished the Judge.

"EXCEPT, I thought that Jay meant, he and the Deputies and the Louisiana Marshals who were, at that point in our Parish. Not alone, my boy! Your turn Jay"– Said the Judge.

"Well, I need a little sherry." Jay said with his cracked, weak voice! el Rico poured glasses of sherry all around to the grown-ups. Sassy poured Root Beer for the Kids. "Huh!!!" Grunted Josh, "Sassy, and Lil' Wolf took a glass of Root Beer, too!"

Henry gave Josh a look that could burn from them blue-green eyes of his.

"Sorry Unk." Said Josh. "O.K. boys." Smiled Henry.

The 'sweet little girls just said, "Thank You, Sassy!"

Jay cleared his throat and started his story ---

"Well," a sip of sherry, "I saddled up my horse as the Judge wrote the Orders – Twelve (12) hours leave and let the three (3) men go to the barn for their horses – pay the nights' fee for the horses' night and care they received. Mad as hornets they were! The Fine charged by the Judge was $10.00 each. MAD! MAD! MAD! and BROKE! They were." Said Jay.

"They left town as quiet as a 'cat stalking a Mouse' – an attitude change, I can tell you," said Jay.

"I followed them, out of sight; I could tell where they were headed. I had muffled Little Paint's hoofs not to make a sound through the woods.

"We went deep into the darkness of the giant oak trees where brush and leaves covered the ground. They doubled back a time or two – to stop anyone following them. I know a trick or two also, AND I know those woods where we hunt all the time! Anyway – in a little while, we were deep in the soundless woods, not a peep, not a grunt from wild hogs, no deer in sight either."

"Somber. Then all of a sudden – I see trampled grass under foot, a trail, noise, talking, and the clash of glass!"

"There it is – The Still - a great cistern on stilts and another and another. A shed made of oak boards, a yard full of wooden barrels with a roof of Palmettos Plants sheltering them from sun and rain!

"An area of leaves and straw needles in the center, and under the cisterns, were cases of glass bottles. What an operation! I had never seen a still before, much less an entire factory site!"

"Well, Little Paint whinnied at the sights and sounds of water running the stills and the heat was on!" Moaned Jay.

"About twenty men on the ground looked at the Giant Oak, moss hanging to the ground; I had taken shelter behind, me and a thirsty Paint" Whimpered Jay.

"I turned Paints' head towards home and ran like hell for the woods leading toward town. Well, the three men I had followed out there were still on horseback and mounted. They whipped their poor horses with a stick – one horse ran head long into a big sapling and got thrown about ten feet into the air and hit the ground hard. I didn't wait to see this show, but I heard it and the men who were airing their opinions, I never heard such language in my life, in Spanish. Thank goodness."

Jay continued, "Anyway I high tailed it out of there, but I took a wrong turn back to town and I ran into the other two men. They shot poor Paint out from under me and I fell, and the Horse, Saddle and all fell on top of me. Poor little Paint was heavy as hell. (Sorry, Ms Amy) The men shot Paint again in the head and left me for dead or close enough. They didn't want to leave a bullet in me because the Judge and the Deputies and Marshalls would come after them.

"Well, I lay there, couldn't move. Night was falling – Wolves were whooping and calling the pack for a feast in the forest! ME! The leader of the pack came closer and closer – I don't remember much after that – except – I pulled my rifle away from my saddle and held the trigger down time after time. I heard a few whelps, but I couldn't get any more bullets from my leather pouch, it was under Poor Paint. I passed out from the pain from my arm and leg where Paint was pinning me down – Thank God my lights went out!" Jay paused.

"I heard a commotion a few minutes later and the pressure of Paint was being lifted off my legs and arm and I felt a dragging pain over my shoulders, face, and head. I must have passed out at that time. I don't remember anything after that, until I was waiting for you to open the damn door. (Sorry, Amy) I have never been in so much pain and lived." Said Jay, making the most serious point he could make.

Henry cleared his throat and looked around at the company and said, "I don't know about you all but this is a mystery to end all mysteries unless we have someone in this room that came here on purpose, to help us learn what happened next."

Henry's eyes circled the room and to his amazement, Lil' Wolf was getting to his feet and was holding his eyes to Henry's, as if to say. "It is my turn; I know the story and the ending of this great mystery, of what has happened to our friend, our Judge, and our town."

Yes, it was his turn.

Henry looked at Jay and said, "Do you remember who was in the forest and helped you, Jay?"

"Not any idea, Henry, it happened on my part, just as the Judge and I told it. But, I do believe our great friend, Lil' Wolf, can add to this mystery, and I, for one, am most anxious to hear his side this story. Lil' Wolf, will you help us to understand how this mystery came to have landed on Henry's front porch?"

Lil' Wolf, stood up, arranged his leather cream colored pants and shirt with the tassels' of colored beads hanging down from his sleeves, and began his story.

"Thank you my friend. I can help you with the rest of this story, as sad as it is. I am glad I was there, when, and where, Jay needed my help. It happened this way."

Lil' Wolf began his part in the mystery.

"I was asleep when I heard the Great Wolf calling to his pack. I took my clothes with me as I opened the flap of my Fathers' Tee Pee. I did not want to wake them by coming back inside to get my clothes in case I needed them. As I stepped outside, I knew by the Great God Warrior above, that someone was in great need of help on this golden night of Moon and Stars shinning above. I ran for 'Warrior' my smallest pony. He was strong, fast, and quiet."

Lil' Wolf continued, "I was deep in the woods when a shooting star brightened the area with a yellow glow of light. I could see a horse hurt or dead not too far from where I had stopped Warrior. I swung down to the floor of the forest from my horse and walked silently to the horse that was down on the ground. It was Jay's horse. I bent down to feel her nose, it was dry. She was dead. Then I noticed that Jay was pinned under Paint and he was 'out like a light.' Paint was not a big horse, but, a horse of any size is very heavy and Paint was a dead weight on top of Jay.

"I was too deep in the woods for any of the Chitimacha Tribe to hear me shout. And I didn't know who else might be close at hand in the woods to hear my call for help. I couldn't leave Jay; the wolves were always close to any injured animal in the forest. They were stalking around us even then. I had to pull Jay out from under Paint. Warrior and I could do it in time.

"Jay did not come to, so I worked as quickly as I could. I took the saddle from Paint and left the blanket between him and Jay for some protection for Jay as I pulled him from under his horse. Warrior had heavy ropes on his head for me to hold onto as I rode him. I used these ropes to pull Jay from under his horse. There was no way Warrior and I could lift Paint from over Jay. We had to do the best we could to get him out as quickly as we could. I had no idea of how long Jay had been pinned under Paint.

"I had only one horse with me. I tied Warrior on to Jay's belt and then caught his shoes in a triangle of ropes to help pull all together and not hurt Jay too much by pulling him apart. I was sweating bullets. Warrior is a very strong horse. He pulled while I guided Jay as best I could from under his horse's body.

"As Warrior and I dragged Jay clear of Paint, I raised him up to lay across Warrior's back and I tied Paint's bridle to my arms and belly and across Warriors head and ears. Warrior was too tired to carry Jay and me to Henry's farm where I was headed.

"I didn't know if I could get Jay to Henry's in time for Henry to help him, but I would try. My big-hearted Warrior ran as fast as I did. We were both very tired and worried about Jay. When I reached Henry's lawn it was almost dawn. The big house was in darkness. I knew what I had to do to save Jay and Warrior, who was almost stopped because he had used all his energy helping me and Jay. I was very worried about my horse, at this time.

"I stopped Warrior, just before the steps of the big porch. I untied Jay and slide him on the top step. Then I pulled him up and stood him next to me. I carried him to the big doors of the house. I was able to lean him against the door, for just a minute or two. That was his limit to stay there.

"I knocked softly at first. Then I thought, 'no one could hear, in time to get to Jay.' So I 'BANGED' on the door. I heard Henry talking to Ms Amy and the door flew open. Henry was too startled to see me drop to the floor and back down the steps to catch Warrior by the bridle I had over his head. I lead him to Henry's barn which has everything to help horse and man. I fed and watered Warrior; I brushed him and hugged him. Henry's good food and fresh water did the trick. It revived Warrior enough to get him home where he could rest. I walked him all the way home. I took the short cut and we made it back safe and sound. We were beat. I nursed him for a day or two and he is well again; we will hunt another day, Warrior and I", Lil' Wolf said proudly.

He continued, "Today, I had to come and see if Jay survived Henry's surgery. I didn't know how badly hurt he was or if he survived the mess he was in. So, I am here, my friends. You look much banged up, as the whites say. But you made it, with Henry's help. May God bless you with all long life."

"No more whiskey stills for you, my friend." Laughed Lil' Wolf and the children.

"Lil' Wolf, I knew you as a great hunter, warrior, and friend. Now I know you as you are, ALL HEART my good and faithful friend. Thank you from the bottom of my heart. I will always be there for you when you need me or just to enjoy our friendship." Said Henry.

"You did well my dear friend. You saved Jay and didn't let our enemy win this round. Sweet and gentle friend thank you and Warrior for all you have done for our family and friends. As you know, you are always welcomed here, with your family and friends." Smiled Henry.

"And I know I speak for the rest of my family, and of course, the Judge and Jay. But they can speak for themselves." Said Henry.

"Hear, hear," said the Judge and Jay and all of the company in that room that day.

Lil' Wolf bowed his head deeply, shook hands with Henry, Jay, and the Judge, and went outside to the wild wind spaces and his horses and woods.

"El Rico, please help Bud and I put Jay in bed where he can rest." Said Henry.

Henry motioned the children follow him into the hall.

"Josh and Ben, you and the cousins go meet Mom and Ms Bessie in the kitchen and they will have lunch ready for you. Ask Sassy to bring Mr. Jays' and Marshals' lunches to the bedroom. Thank you."

"When you have finished your lunch, please go outside and play quietly for a while. You can swing on the swing until Jay is ready for a nap. It has been a hard day for him and everyone. Please do not talk about this story you have heard today. It is very serious. Don't mention it to anyone else! Keep it to yourselves. Thank You." Said Uncle Henry.

Maddie and Bella were quietly crying, hiding behind their hands.

"Yes, Uncle, we understand, is it all right if we go walk under the Oak and Pecan trees for a while?"

"Yes Josh, that is a good place to sit and reflect, just think about what you have heard here today!"

"Go now and get your lunch with the Uncles and Mom, I will be in, in a minute."

Henry wanted to check on Jay and make sure he was doing O.K. and would take a nap after he finished his lunch. Jay was tired, but asked Henry to come talk with him after their rest.

Henry agreed as he shook the trembling hand of his good friend.

Henry and the Judge joined the family in the dining room for a much needed meal. There was a somber air to the meal. After the meal prayer was said, all quieted down to eat and think.

The Judge took to his room for a rest before heading back to town and the Court House.

Lunch was over, the cowboys and farm hands had a much needed rest from the hottest part of the day.

Ms Bessie and Sassy walked upstairs to their rooms to rest, as well.

The family was at rest also. Quietness filled the hot air of the house and farms alike.

The animals rested as well. Hum, yawn.............

The Mystery was solved. Thank God for Lil' Wolf, a mighty Brave and his horse.

It was quiet that evening on the front porch. The children were in their white gowns ready to recite the Rosary and thank God for His miracles' and His Angels.

Good Night Dear Friends.

Chapter Five

"GHOST"

Bailey, Ethel M.T.

One night all was quiet. It was around 1:30 A.M. in the morning. Everyone in the tall three-story Colonial home was fast asleep.

All of a sudden the front door flew open. The door was in the hall, just left of the dining room. Amy's bedroom was at the head of the stairs on the second floor hall of the Mansion. The servants and staff slept on the third floor.

Amy woke up with a start! What was happening? What was that noise coming from the downstairs hall?

"Henry, Josh, Noah, Ben, el Rico?" Amy called to the men and boys of the family. They may be going fishing early today, 'Hum, not this early' thought Amy, looking at the old clock on the mantel.

Then she heard heavy, slow, dragging footsteps coming toward the stairs. One, two, three, four, and five. Heavy, dragging, footsteps. Then a low gurgling, breathing, sound was heard by a very scared Amy.

Amy then heard heavier, deliberate, s l o w footsteps going along the wide up-stairs hall toward the girls bedrooms. One, two, three.

'No mistake there,' thought a mad Amy.

Amy grabbed her pistol and checked the revolving barrel to be sure it held all six bullets. It was loaded; she took the safety lock off.

She picked up the glass chimney lamp that was filled with kerosene liquid. She lit the wick with the matches that were always next to her bed on the night table.

Amy was ready for trouble, no matter what! Nobody was going to hurt her girls, or boys, for that matter.

Amy went slowly to the head of the stairs; all was quiet, too quiet. She took one step at a time; down the long hall. She did not want to warn anyone that she was coming.

The loaded gun was held in front of her in her right hand while the lamp was held in her left.

Amy finally reached the end of the hall; she could hardly breathe.

NOTHING! Nobody was in the Hall!

She slowly went first to Madeline's room on the right hand side of the hall. She turned slowly all around the room. NOBODY!!

Maddie was sound asleep. 'Like a little Angel,' thought Amy looking at her beautiful daughter. Her long dark hair covered her lacey white pillow. She was covered with a quilt with pretty hand-stitching that was made for her last summer by the ladies of the family, friends, and kitchen and household workers.

"Oh dear, my thoughts are straying from the trouble in the house. Not now, tonight!" moaned Amy. She had more important things to do than think about her sweet Maddie's blanket.

Amy checked Madeline's balcony to her room; the double French Doors were shut tight. Amy unlocked them and looked at the balcony. She looked under the bed and in the wardrobe.

'No, nobody there either.' Thought Amy.

Then Amy crossed the hall and made her way to sweet little Belle's room. She slowly opened the door that had been left open a crack to Maddie's hallway and room. Bella was not a scaredy-cat, she would tell you with her big blue eyes looking into yours, she just knew how scared Maddie would be if she did not see Bella's lamp burning a little beam across the hall. Maddie is big enough not to need a lamp turned down low at night as she is a big girl, but, here was Bella saying, no, Maddie needed that little light at night.

Amy checked Bella's closet and behind the heavy drapes and under the bed and the balcony again. Bella had a set of French Doors to the balcony she and Maddie shared. They gave tea parties for the cousins out there; giggles were heard all over the Plantation. Only the girls were invited, of course.

They liked watching the horses and chickens or just sitting at the little tea table and talking. Ms Bessie would sit with them in the afternoon sipping her coffee and teaching them how to knit. Amy taught them how to crochet.

Amy checked the other bedrooms and the boys. She checked the sewing room and the bathing room and the washing up room. Nobody was anywhere. "Except the ones who were supposed to be there." Whispered Amy to herself.

After re-checking the front door and the lock, which was still set, she went back to bed.

'Dreaming?' Thought Amy,

She set the loaded pistol on the pillow next to her head. She still was not at all convinced that someone had not come into the house and left.

"Whew," said Amy with a sigh of relief. "I don't know what I heard, but I am not dreaming! There was someone, or something, coming into this house tonight."

Amy was not able to sleep until it was nearly dawn. She slept deeply for a few hours. UNTIL----

Ms Bessie came into her room softly, carrying a tray of coffee to Amy's bed. Ms Bessie saw the pistol lying on the other pillow. Amy was sound asleep until she caught the smell of fresh-brewed coffee on the tray Ms Bessie was setting on the little table by the bed.

"My, My!" whispered Ms Bessie. "First time in years I caught you in bed in time for me to serve your coffee in bed." Amy sat up and looked at Ms Bessie in her room so early in the morning, to serve her coffee in bed.

They both looked at each other and began to smile and then to laugh out Loud.

"Whoop, Ms. Amy, what has happened to your early morning clock," laughed Bessie, clapping her hands together.

"Good morning Bessie. I must say this is pretty nice and feels real good to get coffee in bed once again and how that coffee smells good," said Amy smiling at Bessie.

The bedroom door flew open and there stood Henry with a puzzled frown on his face.

"Good Morning, Mama, Ms Bessie. Mama are you ill? What has happened to you? It's almost six o'clock!" exclaimed Henry.

"And why on earth are you sleeping with a gun on the other pillow near your head?" Asked an agitated Henry.

"Hush, Hush, you two." Said Mama. "You will wake the children this early in the morning."

"The strangest thing happened in the middle of the night, or early this morning." Said a puzzled Amy.

"Sit down and I will tell you what happened. Oh, Ms Bessie please ask Sassy to bring three more cups of coffee for Henry, yourself, and me. We need coffee for the telling of this happening during the night." Said Amy.

"I'll be just a minute, Ms Amy," said Ms Bessie as she went through the door to catch Sassy in the hall as she was going to the kitchen.

"Please Sassy, bring another tray of coffee into Ms Amy's room for three." Asked Ms Bessie.

"Yes, Mam." Smiled Sassy. There were not too many times that Sassy got to serve her loving mother Ms Bessie.

Mama looked at Henry and shook her head and began to cry, a small choking sound. Mama never cried in front of anyone.

'This is serious,' thought Henry. He sat down on the side of Amy's bed to comfort her. The curtains were slowly blowing from the ceiling to floor windows in the early morning breeze coming from the bayou.

Bessie gave a little tap on the door before entering the room.

"Sassy is bringing fresh coffee in just a minute. Now, now Ms Amy, what is all this fuss about? You been crying? Well, I never!" Ms Bessie was speaking low and slowly. She was used to a very strong, in command, Mistress.

'This is really bad,' thought Bessie.

"Well," sighed Amy. This is what happened last night. She began to tell them what had taken place in the house after midnight when everyone was asleep."

Beginning with the big front door banging open.

Henry felt his hair stand straight up on the back of his neck. While listening to Mama's horrible story of last night.

Ms Bessie was wide eyed and her mouth was working, but nothing was coming out. She was going into shock. In total disbelieve of such a thing happening here.

'This is bad,' thought Ms Bessie, 'totally bad and evil'.

"What does it mean?" asked Henry in total puzzlement, worry, and anger.

The lines in Henry's face and brows were in constant turmoil. He began clenching his hands into a fist. Then he would unclench and clench again, over and over.

Mama was quiet, very quiet, sipping her coffee, holding the fragile cup cradled in both hands. Her eyes were bright and deep in thought.

"Mama, listen," said Henry putting his arms around his mother's shoulders and kissing her hair.

"Would you agree to my calling a Soiree (a visit) this evening after six o'clock, with the adults of the family and telling them of this experience? They may know something of what we are talking about and have some ideas as to how to approach this intrusion into our home, in the middle of the night." Suggested Henry, while looking at his Mother and Ms Bessie.

"Yes, honey, we agree with you." said Mama looking at Ms Bessie for confirmation.

"We will carry on today, just like any other day, and catch a little time to talk amongst ourselves the best we can. While having our tea, we can get our thoughts in order for tonight." Replied Amy.

"Henry, please be careful that the boys are not around when we are carrying on a conversation about this mystery. Maybe at their nap time would be a good time to have a short discussion. The girls do not need to know of this either. What do you think?" Asked Amy.

"I agree," said Henry.

"Oh, Henry, please ask Jo Ed to tell Taunti' Eloise, that someone will pick her up in the buggy around four- thirty this evening. I want to visit with her during dinner and awhile before the others come in. I haven't seen her in a week," Said Amy.

"Sure, Mom, I think she will enjoy the attention and the visit. This kind of mystery falls right into her hands, being, an' Trémater', a Treater, of small illnesses and fever, little and large slivers and such. She treats the patient with prayers. She is also good at solving little puzzles and mysteries of the dark side of daily living." Smiled Henry.

"I asked Charlie to come out too. He will be having dinner and staying the night."

"We are always happy to have Charlie. He is welcome anytime, son." Agreed Amy.

"Thank you, Mom. Charlie and I know that."

The days' work went on as usual. The men worked in the field preparing them for a new crop of corn, sugar cane, rice, and string beans, as they were the main crops.

Other fields were plowed as well. The fields of vegetables were planted early. Then the sugar cane was laid one short piece after the other to be watered and soon the little stalks of new plants could be seen for miles around.

Corn was an important crop for the Louisiana Planters as well. It was called the "Cash Crop." The farmers could harvest the sweet ears of corn and bring them to market by the wagon loads. Everyone loved boiled corn on the cob or shucked the corn to add to soups and stews.

The children gathered eggs and fed the chickens. They drew water from the big cistern in the back yard into buckets to add fresh water in the troughs for the cows and horses to drink.

Josh could see Wayne laying salt-lick bricks all over the pastures where the cattle were penned for them to lick them whenever they needed salt in their diet. Other workers were doing the same thing in the other pastures for every farm animal, mules, cows, horses, and goats that roamed the pastures and ate the sweet grass that grew there.

The children went to visit with Jay on the front porch. He had occupied the swing from the day Henry said he could get out of bed for a while. Sassy and Ms Bessie piled on pillows and a quilt covered the seat of the swing.

"Huh," Said Henry, "I'd never get that kind of treatment".

"Oh hush, Henry, the girls enjoy spoiling him and to see how he is improving every day." Said Amy.

"Well I guess, but you see how much he enjoys the ladies waiting and making over him." Whined Henry.

"Oh, son, I will have them do the same thing, if and when, you are in his condition, I promise." Laughed Amy

"Mom, never mind! I just hope I am never in that "condition". Jay deserves all the attention and good care he is getting with us." Said Henry.

"Coffee time, Ms. Amy and Mr. Henry, if you're ready." Said Ms Bessie as she opened the porch- screened door.

Sassy had the tray of coffee all ready to give to Ms Bessie to serve the grownups sitting on the porch. Sassy followed Ms Bessie with a tray of root beer made for the children sitting on the steps.

"Hey, Madeline!" shouted Josh, "Come join us! We got root beer Sassy made for us! Come on Maddie and Bella, hurry!"

The two girls sitting on the balcony were reading a book each taking turns reading a chapter apiece when it was their turn. They read many books that way.

"O. K. Josh!" yelled Madeline, save us some of that root beer. "Madeline and Bella were soon heard running down the stairs to the big hall in the front of the house.

Bella almost fell over Madeline, as Maddie slowed down just before she reached the last two steps of the stairs. Maddie knew, and Bella had to learn, that young ladies of a certain age, with good manners and who came from a good family, were accepted into the social society of New Orleans.

These were Amy's Rules: Young Ladies do not run, jump, and sweat like tomboys after they reach the age of ten years old and young Ladies were expected to have good manners and be polite.

Madeline and Bella caught their breath at the bottom of the landing and walked onto the front porch. They kissed Amy, Uncle Henry, and Mr. Jay, good morning and sat in rockers to wait for their root beer. They didn't have to wait long. Sassy came out with fresh lemonade and root beer for all who were sitting on the porch enjoying the company and the sunshine.

Josh, Noah, and Ben were sitting on the steps enjoying their drinks and watching Madeline; she usually had something up her sleeve for Uncle Henry to sort out.

They were right. A few minutes later she looked at Uncle Henry and smiled and said, "Uncle Henry, are you taking the boys fishing tomorrow? Bella and I would like to go to. Huh Bella?"

"Not me!" Said Bella. I am afraid of the hook, the snakes, the water, and the jokes the boys play on us. Don't you remember Maddie? The last time we went fishing we ran all the way home, like scared rabbits." Said Bella, "No Way" she added.

"You are so right Bella. How could I forget that?" Said Maddie. "We're staying home. We can have a picnic with the cousins, Susie, Kathy, and Grace can come. Huh Mama." Asked a sweet Maddie.

"I think so Maddie, that's a good idea. Send word to the cousins. We can bake a cake for them." Finished Amy.

"CAKE!" yelled Ben, who always wants cake. "We get cake in our basket, too?" he asked.

"Sure," said Mama," A big cake goes a long way, huh Ms Bessie? We will bake a chocolate one."

"Well, I'll put my bid in for chocolate cake, too." Said Jay.

"Count me in on that one, too." Said Henry.

"Well, look there, Jerome and Sam have finished all the chores for the day while we sat here swinging and talking time away."

"Jerome, Sam, come join us for root beer and lemonade on the porch," said Amy

"Thanks Ms. Amy sounds good to us."

"I will send Sassy with a fresh tray of glasses. I'll go check on supper." Said Amy, getting out of her rocker.

"Henry will you help me carry these trays back into the kitchen, please", Said Amy.

"Yes, Mama." Replied Henry.

As Amy got into the Hall and then went into the library, dragging Henry with her.

She said, "Henry, the visit of the family and friends is at seven o'clock. Can we please recite the Rosary and then we will eat and get the kids to bed, then get ready for the family visit. O.K."? Asked Amy.

"O. K. Mom, everyone sitting on the porch is coming to the visit tonight. Do we have something to serve, to eat?" Asked Henry.

"Yes, honey, we have finger sandwiches, cookies, and muffins with coffee and lemonade.

"That sounds good, Mom. I will be ready. I will get the boys settled. Maddie will help Bella. All's taken care of early enough for tonight. I'll get my Rosary while I'm in here. Oh, I'll get Jay's too. Jerome and Sam carry their Rosaries in a pocket with them. I'll light some candles too. I know Sassy will have a lantern or two. We will meet in the living room, O.K. Mom?" Asked Henry.

Jerome and Sam went home to their supper and to get ready for the visit concerning last night's mysterious visitor.

The table was set in the dining room for supper. The boys, Madeline, and Bella were in their white gowns. They all looked like angels.

Henry said "Ben, please say the Blessing."

Everyone bowed their heads for the Blessing.

Ben began, "Bless Us, Oh Lord, and these Thy gifts, which we are about to receive through Thou bounty of Christ, Our Lord. Amen."

The meal was one of Ms Bessie's favorites: Baked Ham, sweet potatoes, lima beans, fresh bread and sweet tea or water.

The family finished their meal, stood up, and said the Meal Prayer in thanksgiving for this wonderful meal.

The family went to the porch. The children sat on the swing and the adults sat in the easy rocking chairs. Henry went down and sat on the top step, where he could see the moon, while they prayed the Rosary.

They finished the Rosary and went up to bed. Well, all except those who were going to the Soiree tonight.

Henry and Gloria, the children's maid and housekeeper, saw that the children were all set upstairs. The Nanny brought a book to read to them. Henry had brought a pitcher of water to put in their bedrooms. He tucked the boys in for the night and then checked on Madeline and Bella. They were all settled and Maddie was reading a story to Bella.

Henry went to his room for a few minutes of peace before meeting with the family. After his bath, he decided to put on his gown and smoking jacket then he would be ready for bed. That little luxury made him feel better about the meeting tonight; he can just crawl into bed after the meeting.

Oh, what a great thing to look forward to. Rest. Henry was almost asleep, sitting on the bed, putting on his slippers. Comfort and sleep was all that Henry was thinking of.

Then Henry thought of Charlie, where was Charlie? It's getting dark and Charlie has had too many bad experiences in the dark. That's because he is a 'Rich Boy' and looks it. I'll send Sam and Joel to check on him along the trail to town.

el Rico softly knocked on Henry's door and let himself in. Henry looked really tired this evening. el Rico had been getting Jay ready for the night. He helped him with his bath, the shaving process, getting into his gown, and then into bed. el Rico just wanted to check on Henry to see if he needed anything before he went to bed.

Henry went looking for Jerome to ask him to get Sammy and Joel to look for Charlie, who had not shown up yet. He then went looking for Amy, who was in the kitchen with Bessie and Sassy. They were making rolls and sandwiches.

Amy was fine, so he went into the living room. It is really a beautiful room. The room had four ceiling to floor windows, the frames were stained a deep Walnut. There were two big French Doors that went out to the big garden porch. There were lots of plants, flowers, potted trees, lanterns and Lamps.

At this point, Henry remembered that Jay wanted to be in on the Soiree tonight. So he went looking for Amy to tell her before anyone got settled in the living room, of Jay's request.

Amy agreed and didn't know why she hadn't thought of it.

They told Jerome about the change to Jay's room instead of in the living room. So everyone was directed to Jay's room for the Soiree tonight.

A buggy drove up in front on the drive and Henry went down to help Taunti' Eloise into the room where they were meeting. Henry introduced Taunti' Eloise to Jay and they realized they knew each other from a funeral they both attended.

Jimmy, Francis, Willie, Jerome, and the family came in.

An old friend of the family, Mr. Savant, came with his Valet Cliff, and sat near Taunti' Eloise and Jay.

"Where is Charlie?" Worried Henry. No word from the two men that were sent out to find him. Another mystery.

Everyone was here. Coffee and finger sandwiches and rolls were passed.

Amy started her story. "In the middle of the night, the front opened with a bang. A shuffling sound came across the big hall. I was sleeping in the bedroom at the top of the stairs. I came out with my gun and followed the sound going toward the front of the hall, toward the double French doors, to the outdoor Balcony."

"I was shaking like a leaf," said Amy. "I went to look after the girls and the boys sleeping down the hall. Nobody was there. I did not see anyone leave. No one passed me in the hall and I didn't see anyone in the house.

But, I know I heard dragging footsteps and there was mud all over the hall and the stairs. Walter helped me clean it up. I didn't ask anyone else to help. I hope whoever it was comes back here tonight for us to solve this mystery." Finished Amy.

Amy looked around the room to Taunti' Louisa', but no. She was shaking her head and raised the palms of her hands upwards to indicate that she didn't know what was happening either.

Amy then looked at Jay. No, nothing. At Henry, at the Uncles and the servants. Nobody had anything to say about the mystery.

Amy faced Mr. Savant, an old friend.

Amy's eyes stopped at Mr. Savant. The look of horror on his face frightened her. His hands were hands of a skeleton. His stiff-bolted-upright body, added pain to her tired body.

"Mr. Savant, would you like a little water? What is it?" Asked Amy.

Henry left his chair and went to stand by Amy. He signaled Bud and Jim to go stand by Mr. Savant's chair for now. They went to do as requested.

Mr. Savant opened his eyes, after he had them closed for a few seconds.

He looked at Amy and he said, "Amy, you must be very brave. What you have encountered, by no fault of your own, is a slave from the dead." Mr. Savant had tears in his eyes and his hands were held in an attitude of prayer.

And then he said, "This ghost has lost his life to guard the treasures of the slave owner of this plantation in 1862. When the man who owned this plantation knew his home would be plundered and destroyed because of the nature of the men of the North, these men invaded our town and were soldiers fighting in the Civil War.

"One afternoon these men rode into town on Main street and shot, in cold blood, three old men sitting on the front porch of the bakery who were just smoking and visiting with each other, a daily routine of theirs. They were friends of mine," Said a sad Mr. Savant

He continued, "The owner of this plantation had a slave, bigger than anyone. He was known as the 'Gentle Giant'. The owner called him Sam; they were friends. The owner and Sam gathered together to pick and choose and carry the treasure of the House of Idle Wile' into the yard. They would bury the grant to the property, the jewels, silver and gold coins, the diamonds, and China ware under the pecan trees that dotted the Plantation."

"After the choices had been made, Mr. Arrington asked Sam to go get an old man, or whomever he chose, to be shot and buried to keep the treasure safe until they came back home again.

"Sam looked at Mr. Arrington and said, 'Boss, it is me. I choose to guard your treasure. I can do this. I do not want to be a prisoner of the Yankees. I am petrified most of that. So shoot me now and cover the grave. You can take care of my family until the end has come.' There were shots in the air; Sam's eyes were red in fear.

"O.K. Sam." said Mr. Arrington. And he shot him in the head with the 32 Revolver from his hip. 'Oh Sam.' said Mr. Arrington, 'I will miss you much more than that cold gold.'

"Then he made a rough map and directions of the site marking where they buried the treasure. He put the map in Sam's pocket. As for remembering the location of the treasure, he was sure that he could find it again if he survived the War between the Northern Yankees and the Southern Rebels.

"I can tell you why Sam is coming above ground after all these years. May I have a cup of coffee, please?" Mr. Savant asked.

"Of course, Mr. Savant, I am so sorry you had to ask. Here is Ms Bessie with a fresh cup take a while, have your coffee and rest, Sir, before continuing with the story." Said Henry.

"We are all spell-bound. I never imagined such a thing happening, especially because we live in this house and the house has a Ghost." Amy said.

"Well Amy, I am ready to go on as he may come back tonight." Said Mr. Savant

He began again, "The Arrington family, and the families of their slaves, all went with the Master. They took the train to Oklahoma where Mrs. Arrington was from. Her family had a lot of houses in Oklahoma, so all of Mr. Arrington's family and the families of his Slaves were welcome there."

Mr. Savant looked at Amy and said, "Amy, when you hear the ghost again tonight, get your gun, you can't really use it against a ghost, but it will give you strength. Sam will not harm you; however, it will be scary to meet a ghost from a grave that was dug so many years ago.

"Sam will go to you. Stand in the hall where Henry can come to your aid if you need him. But Henry! You must stay in bed as if you are sleeping. Sam only wants to talk to Ms. Amy. That is who he has chosen to come out to.

"When Sam comes into the door, just be calm, he is looking for you. He knows you. I don't know how, but what Sam wants is to be relieved from his responsibility of the treasure that is chained to him. He is looking for you to release him of his burden. What you do is, when you see Sam come in, just ask Sam this question, 'SAM, Give me your Burdon"

Mr. Savant continued, "Sam will give you a map to where the treasure is buried. Sam will then leave to follow his Soul. This is what he has been longing for. Sam is in a state between the walking dead and devils without souls. Their souls are not with them. Only God knows why this is so and where the souls are."

That night Amy sat up in a beautiful gray chair until she heard the big door open and slam. 'Hard again,' thought Amy. She got up trembling and walking forward, holding onto each piece of furniture, she traveled to the front hall where only God knows what was looking for her. She heard the five footsteps again and the sound of the dragging feet.

AND there he was! As Amy had a good look at this horrible, smelly, and terrible thing in front of her, she shook like a leaf from a tree in a hard, high wind. The look of the walking-dead giant of a man in front of her stunned her senses.

Her voice was croaky as she opened her mouth to speak to him. "Sam, Sam, give me your Burdon."

In a gust of a hot wind Sam vanished, leaving his torn, worn out smelly and muddy clothes behind him on the floor of the hall.

Lying on the floor by Amy was a dirty, worn, piece of paper. Amy picked it up with another piece of whole paper, where it rested on the clean paper like a leaf about to crinkle apart.

Amy quickly put it in an envelope, she had ready for this purpose.

A Historian could help them with this historic note. He could even copy it. 'Thank God.' Thought Amy.

Henry, Jerome, and el Rico came down stairs to comfort Amy and get her a cup of tea to recover her sense, after such a weird and unholy experience.

Henry walked Amy to bed. el Rico brought in a sweet cup of tea, and Henry added a little Sassafras to help her sleep.

"Henry, please say a decade of The Rosary for Sam's safe passage to God." Asked Amy.

"Yes, Mom. Close your eyes and el Rico and I will pray out loud." said Henry, who was sad to see that his Mother had to go through this experience to save a Soul from the Past.

Henry, Jerome, and el Rico went into the Library for a glass of Sherry or Whiskey to calm them down and help them sleep. Jerome did the honors for the tired, sleepy friends sitting in the Library.

"Henry, Henry." A loud voice from outside came to the men's ears.

"el Rico, please go see who is out there. Jerome will help you, and I need to see if the noise woke up Mom." Said Henry. 'However,' he thought, as he walked to Amy's room, now that he had a minute to think on it, 'Charlie had not emerged from the forest or the trail all night.' He recognized that voice, it had to be Charlie, finally showing up. 'I wonder what happened to him?' thought Henry as he entered into Amy's room just as his mother was getting out of bed again. Thought Henry, 'Oh No.'

"Mom, stay in bed, honey, its Charlie finally showing up for the evening." Henry kissed his Mother on the forehead and covered her up again to say 'Good night.' However, Amy would not hear of such a thing.

"Henry, let me up! I have got to see Charlie and then I'll go back to bed," promised Amy.

"O.K. Mama, let me settle you down into a nice big chair in the Library and we will bring Charlie in there, so you won't miss a thing." Smiled Henry. As he left his Mother and went to the big porch to see Charlie.

el Rico had a hold of Charlie trying to lead him up the steps of the Great House.

"Charlie, we are glad you made it. We sent out two men to look for you but you were nowhere to be seen. Where have you been?" Asked Henry as he maneuvered Charlie into the big Hall.

"Henry, I got off track to Idle Wile' this afternoon by Louisa' and Katherine's. They needed an escort to the Roosevelt for a Tea and Meeting of the Rex Parade participants with the King of Rex and the Captain of the Crew. Their Mother and Father were delayed at the farm in Plaquemines by the President Paddle Wheeler docking there to have a 'show and peek', at a real Southern Plantation Home.

"They were caught by the Captain of the Boat, who is a good friend and has done many and various favors for them and their family and friends."

"So, of course, I couldn't leave the girls at the Hotel. I had to wait with them during the meeting, luncheon and tea until their parents could get to the Hotel. And they were late!"

"I felt like Sir Galahad. Man am I tired. Show me a whiskey and a bed." Said Charlie, who was not kidding.

"el Rico, if you aren't too tired, do you mind taking Mooney to the Stable to the boys to get him feed, water, and a fresh bed of hay. I'll get the whiskey and Charlie's bag from Mooney's saddle and get him a bed upstairs that is already made up for him. Thank you el, please go on to bed after "Sir Charlie's" chores." Laughed Henry.

Well, Charlie, Mom is waiting up for you in the Library, to say Goodnight and to make sure you arrived, safely."

"I am so sorry, Ms. Amy, to keep you up so late." "Apologized Charlie.

He explained what had delayed him.

Amy agreed with Henry, Charlie had done the right thing by being with the girls until their parents arrived at the Hotel.

Then Henry followed Amy back to her bedroom and tucked her into her bed for the night.

Charlie and Henry took their Rosary from their pockets and recited the beads, before they parted for their bedrooms.

Good Night Dear Friends.

Chapter Six

"MARIE LAVEAU"
(the Voodoo Queen)

Bailey Ethel M. T.

Luis, a man known by Henry's friend, Ms K., knows he is dying and needs Sprites, a person who delves into the Spirit World to heal those who are possessed by the Devil.

Luis knows he is possessed.

He said he would die on Monday morning. He has had a spell put on him, by a Cult from Costa Rica, where he came from. Although he is a Roman Catholic, he still believes in this Cult and its powers. He was raised knowing this Cult exists.

Henry wants to call a Doctor to help Ms K's (Ski) friend, Luis but she said that, "A doctor cannot possibly help him. This is Espiritismo".

"Then what is the weapon?" asked Henry.

"The 'Mind" Answered Ms K. ", I don't think you can convict anyone for that." Replied Henry.

"Exactly, which makes it very clever, the perfect crime?" Answered Ms K.

Ms K. and Henry visited the West Indies Botanical Shop on Charters Street in New Orleans. This is the place where they look to identify the Black Congo candle, shaped liked a male figure about six inched tall, found in Luis' room when they visited him as he lay dying.

"It's burned when one hopes for the death of an enemy." Ms K. told Henry.

Other objects found in the shop were statues of the Holy Virgin Mary, a Buda, Holy Medals lying on velvet cloth, herb-burners fashioned of pottery and plastic, bottles advertised as ritual lotions. Antique glass ware, small furniture and shawls and scarves of all kind and color. There were also Rare and secondhand books. The shop cool, clean of clutter and softly lighted with bees wax candles and lamps of kerosene oil.

A bell jingles and jangles as the attendant opened the door for Kathrine and Henry to draw near another door that was covered by a Heavy set of drapes. The attendant pulled back the curtains to reveal a door to the back yard. The yard was bare of grass and contained what looked to be Junk.

Stone jugs, lamps, and innumerable drawings made in chalk or lime stone on the hard-beaten earth around Luis. We had found him.

Meanwhile Thomas, an Altar Boy, was passing in front of Marie's, door, eating from a cup of Ice Cream. She called to him.

"Thomas please take this note to Father Jerry, here is a quarter for you", Mon ami'.

"Merci, Madam Marie" Answered Thomas, and was on his way to St. Ann's Catholic Church.

Father Jerome is the priest delegated by the Ordinary to perform this office. He will first go to Confession, heard by another Priest. If time does not permit, he will say a Perfect Act of Contrition.

Father Jerry will then say The Holy Sacrifice of the Mass and implore God's Help in other fervent prayers.

Here Luis Mendez had been laid out on the earthen floor beside an intricately decorated vertical pole of many carvings and colors. He had been stripped of everything but his white shorts. All kinds of delicate white designs had been drawn on the earth around him. His head was wrapped in a bandage that ran from the top of his head to his jaw, and a second bandage bound his two big toes together. His eyes were open but vacant. Candles were burning at various points of his body. Several lanterns hung from the wall and the ceiling. The air was thick with incenses. Half a dozen people surrounded Madame Laveau.

Marie Laveau

A strange and eerie chill rose at the nape of Henry's neck and traveled across his scalp. The declamatory voice rose and fell like a bird in the hushed and darkening place, Like a hawk or an eagle, he thought beating it's wings against the walls until the walls appeared to recede, disappearing altogether, and he stood in astonishment, centuries removed from New Orleans, listening to a Priestess speak to the Gods.

When the incantations abruptly ended he felt disoriented and confused; he discovered he was sweating profusely for reasons he couldn't understand and which his rational mind could not explain. He stole a glance at his friend, Ms K. and` saw that her eyes were closed and her face serene. as the rituals continued he returned his attention to Madam Leveau, but if what followed seemed to him bizarre and preposterous he didn't smile; he was unable to forget what he had felt during the incantations unable to forget a sense of Presences, of forces appealed to and converging...onto Luis

Luis Mendez lay like a corpse except for an occasional twitching or shouting of what sounded like obscenities.

As Henry watched small piles of food and nuts were distributed at certain points of his body, and just as he wondered why in hell somebody's left over bread and nuts were distributed at certain points of Luis' body, two hens and a rooster were carried into the oum'pour (temple) and given to Madam Leveau, she grasped the chickens under each arm and set them on Luis so they could peck at the food on his body while at the same time she began a curious crossing and uncrossing of Luis' arms, chanting, "Ent, te,te,tete, t..."

When the piles of corn had been reduced in size the chickens were exchanged for the rooster, and Henry felt a stab of alarm. The angry cock left small bloody wounds as it moved up Luis body, heading for his face; barely in time, someone stepped forward to cover the man's eyes. After this cock was carried away and turned loose in the yard outside, lighted candles began to be passed over Luis from head to foot again weaving that same strange pattern while the incantations of Ent, te, te, tete rose in volume.

Abruptly Madam Laveau became silent, and moved over to a basin and gathered up the liquid in her hands and vigorously slapped Luis's face. Others moved in and began to thrash Luis' with water; he was helped to a half-sitting position and whipped with small dripping sacks until the bandages fell away from his dripping body.

Cloves of garlic were thrust into his mouth while Madam Laveau continued to call on the dead sprits to Depart, from Luis' body, her voice rising to a Crescendo of Orders.

Suddenly the door slowly opened and quietly, Father Jerome, a Catholic Priest of St. Ann's Catholic Church, and Thomas, the Altar Boy in His White Alb and carrying a lite white candle in a gold holder, came into the room.

Father Jerome, is the Priest delegated by the Ordinary to perform this office. Father had first gone to Confession and offered the Holy Sacrifice of the Mass, and other fervent prayers, to implore God's help for a person in need. Father wore around his neck, a Blessed Purple Stole.

The room grew silent, except for a moan from Luis' and the restless movement of his legs...

Father Jerome

Marie came to Father's Side and thanked him for replying to her call for help in the case of Luis', a Catholic man.

Marie kissed Father's Ring, in a respectful and welcoming gesture of Peace and Thanksgiving for his presence.

Father than, gave the cross to, Thomas, a sixteen year old Altar Boy, to stand before the people who were there and Luis', to protect them from the Demon's that possess' him.

Father said a few words to Marie and she left his side to pick up a little glass bowl and handed it to Father.

Father is vests in a surplice and purple stole. Having before him the person possessed (who should be bound if there is any danger). Father traces the sign of the Cross over Luis, then over himself and the bystanders, and then sprinkles all of them with Holy Water. After this, he kneels and says the Litany of the Saints, exclusive of the prayers, which follow it. All present are to make the responses.

On this occasion both the Roman Ritual and the Roman Pontifical directed that the first three invocations be repeated. The music for this Litany is given to Anna, the Canter, and whose voice rises to the heavens of the Lord. The invocations are sung by the Canter and responded by all who are present.

P: Lord Have Mercy on us,

All: Lord Have Mercy on us, etc.

Father then invokes all the Saints in Heaven and on Earth to graciously hear us, Oh Lord, and deliver us from evil, Oh Lord. Amen.

"Our Father, Who art in Heaven," Marie and the Altar Boy, Thomas knelt down and the community followed.

When the Prayer was finished, Father took up the chain of the Incense Burner; the Altar Boy, Thomas, filled it with Blessed Incense.

Father then lights the Incense and begins the procession all around the room spreading the Holy Smoke upward toward Heaven and the people and objects it surrounds, so they were One with God. Father slowly walked all around the room and Luis', and friends.

Father Jerome then stooped down and removed his Sandals', Thomas did the same.

Father then said to the people; "Take off your shoes; you are walking on Holy Ground.

When the Ritual was complete, Father and Thomas, and the Community of Friends started the Prayers for the Removal of Demons and Unholy Sprits to leave Luis' and the World.

Father circles Luis', He prayed many Prayers of Demands and Shouts of Orders to the Evil Demons occupying Luis's Body and Mind.

Father made many demands to the Demons and Luis'. Luis' Mouth opened and his eyes caught on fire, his nostrils flared, and his hair stood up on top of his head.

Luis's ears became pointed and at the same time, he spat blood from his open mouth.

A Fire started on Luis' bed. Father sprinkled Holy Water on the fire and it went out.

Father took up the Blessed Oil, and he approached the Bed, a Flash of Lighting and Thunder shook the room. The Community of Friends followed Marie's actions to fall on her knees and with folded hands reaching to God in Heaven, began to pray, 'The Hail Mary', asking the assistance of Our Blessed Mother to intervene for Luis' and themselves.

Father leaned over Luis', and repeated several times, Repent, Repent, Repent, and Luis', Cast out the Devils in your Soul, Mind, and Body.

Luis' began to yell, and Pray the Our Father, and then started his Confession to repent of his sins before God and this Holy Man.

"Bless me Father for I have sinned." His face turned Green. His tongue foamed inside his mouth. Yellow Bile, Oil, and Mud spewed out of his mouth and nose.

Father, Prayed all the harder, Luis' began to sit up and to pray.

Luis' completed his confession of his sins.

"Send the Devil Forth, Luis', you have the Power now! Repent of your sins, your Penance is to say a Rosary a day, and go to Mass on Sunday. I Absolve you, of your sins, In The Name of The Father and of The Son, and of The Holy Spirit." Amen. Prayed Father.

Luis' said the 'Act of Contrition.' Thomas, Marie, Henry, Ms K., and Friends joined in, which filled the room with a very Powerful Prayer.

Father then yelled at Luis'.

"Luis', Cast Out the Demons!"

"You have the Power, Use it Luis'." Demanded Father

Luis' Blew Up, He yelled and screamed and cried and prayed, he was 'A Power of God," He Blew Out the Demons from His Mouth, His Stomach, and His Ears

Luis' was Mad; The Demons were Mad and on Fire, Eyes flashing, Heads on Fire.

Horrible Things, Not of this World, but of the Underworld, The Hole of Fire, and Named HELL.

AND, There was Michael, The Arc Angel, with the Power of His Allegiance with Jesus Christ and His Flaming Sword, fighting the Demons from returning to Earth from the Mouth of Hell, where God had cast them out, centuries ago.

Luis' fell back on his bed.

Father Blessed the Friends of Luis' and He Blessed Marie. He apologized to everyone and invited them to attend Mass in thirty minutes, at Saint Ann's Catholic Church; It was time for the Blessings of The Red Mass for the Fire Men of New Orleans. This is their Church and Father Jerome is their Chaplin.

"Luis' will be fine in a few days of recuperation, Marie/ I leave him to you and your healing hands. Thank you for calling me. Have him and the room cleaned up as soon as you can."

"God Bless you and your friends. I must go."

Father then made the Sign of The Cross before all who were there, Blessing them all.

"In The Name of The Father, And of The Son, and Of the Holy Spirit, Amen.

Father Jerome picked up his bag, the Cross and Thomas, his Altar Boy, followed. His face was very White and he had been crying. Father looked at him and gave him a hug and a kiss on his head.

"Thomas, I will take you home, now, and I will see your Father and Mother right away. I will talk to them of what you have been through. Your Father is a Doctor, and he will know how to treat you for shock of what you have been through, today.

I will pray for you during Mass, Thomas. Thank you for your Help and all you have done, for Jesus, Luis' and I today. You, Thomas, are an Angel of God's.

I will come and see you tomorrow. God Bless You, Son." Said Father.

Father saw Thomas's parents and they were worried, but they knew he had performed a good and Holy Service for God, Father Jerome, and Luis, a poor soul of the Church.

Meanwhile, Luis' suddenly shuddered violently from head to foot and fell back on the cot. He was almost unconscious.

Madam Laveau was finished with the Job of cleaning him and the room up, she and her friends and she leaned over him.

"Luis'", "Luis'", she called. "Luis', is it you?" She asked.

"Yes," he said in a calm and normal voice.

"I think the rest of the Dead Spirits are leaving now." Whispered Ms K., Henry's friend, her eyes bright and intent.

Ms K. and Henry realized all of a sudden, that Marie Laveau was not quiet finished with the Exorcism.

A jar filled with something alcoholic was poured over a stone lying in a dish, and flames sprang up. The streaming dish was carried to Luis' and passed over his body, several times, again describing that same intricate pattern of movement, after which Madam Laveau put it down, seized a bottle of fluid and lifted it to her lips, drank from it several times and each time she SPAT it between her teeth and over Luis'.

"We move out into the yard now." Said Ms K. in a low voice, nudging Henry and he followed her and the others outside to a corner of the enclosure where a deep hole had been dug. To Henry's surprise it had grown dark while they were inside, and the lamps encircling the hole sent bizarre shadows flickering up and down the fence.

He turned to see Luis' limp from the building on the arms of two young men and Luis' approached the illuminated circle, Henry saw that he looked stronger and his eyes were wide open and no longer cloudy. He was carefully helped down into the hole and a tree of equal stature was placed in it beside him. The rooster, protesting was again passed over Luis' body and the incantations began again. At Last, concluding with Madam Laveau calling out in a ringing, down-to-earth voice.

"The Holy Catholic Church and I demand that you return the Life of this Man."

With this she grasped a jug, poured its contents over Luis' Head, broke it with a blow of her fist, and let the pieces fall into the hole. She was still chanting as Luis' was pulled out of the hole. The rooster was placed inside it, instead and buried alive at the foot of the tree.

The Ritual was not over yet, but Henry's gaze was fixed on Luis' now, who was being helped into a long White Gown. He stood unsupported, his skin had color again, and his eyes were bright, no longer haunted. It was unbelievable, when Henry remembered the Prostrate, Gray-Faced, nearly lifeless man he'd seen lying on the Earthen floor only a short while ago.

"He will remain here now, near the Sacred Peristyle for several days." Said Ms K. briskly.

"If the tree dies, Luis' will live. If the tree lives, Luis will die. Only when this is known will he leave here. Dead or Alive."

"Do you understand, Henry?" Asked Ms K.

"Yes," said Henry, still weak in the knees and stunned at what he had just witnessed.

"I understood Father's part and even part of Marie's. I did, I just don't know if I understand them together or apart for that matter. It's a Mystery to me." Said Henry.

"I think the Dead Spirits are leaving now." Whispered Madam Laveau, looking at Henry's friend, her eyes was gleaming and tired.

With a Slow Motion and her head bent down, Marie Laveau, slowly made 'The Sign of The Cross," over Luis' and Henry, Ms K., her people and herself and said, in a warm low voice:

"Thank The Good and Loving Lord for His many Favors. In The Name of The Father and of The Son and of the Holy Spirit. Amen."

All of the people in this group bowed their heads in a prayer, of Thanksgiving. They left the Rest in The Hands of The Great and Good Lord.

Ms K. and Henry bid 'Good Night', to Madam Laveau and her group of friends and left the shop with Aunt Alice and walked toward Henry's horse and buggy that had been brought round from the stables by Kelly.

"Are you alright, Aunt Alice?" Asked Henry of their Chaperone for the Evening.

"Well, Yes Henry, thank you for this evening. I have had this experience before. It is always interesting". Replied Aunt Alice with a tired smile.

"Are you alright, Henry?" Asked Ms K.

"Of course, I'm alright Katherine." Answered Henry, in an effort to sound normal.

'Normal. What is that?' Henry asked himself. 'Will I ever really know what 'Normal" is ever again,' he thought.

As Henry, Ms K., and Aunt Alice rode away, Henry said, "Okay, Explain what just happened."

"Madam Laveau, would be the better person to ask." Katherine yawned as she pointed this out to Henry.

"I can only tell you what she discovered when she visited Luis' in his rooms. She is, you know, a detective in her own way."

"Oh?" Asked a sarcastic Henry.

"She found what she called a 'Disaster Lamp in Luis' back yard." Continued Madam K. Aunt Alice shook her head in agreement.

"We went out, all of us, and in a corner of the yard under a tree, it was obvious that digging had taken place, within the last week.

Ms K. added distastefully, "I must say the lamp was a disaster in itself when we dug it up. It smelled terrible. Madam Savant said it contained the Gall Bladder of an Ox, Soot, Lime Juice, and Castor Oil."

"All right, but how would Luis' know it was there?" Asked Henry.

"Exactly," said Ms K. "Someone, obviously, had to tell him it was there, or send him an added clue or some other type of symbol that was terrifying to Luis'. Madam Savant's guess was that some grave yard dust was sent him through the mail, or left on his doorstep. It would have to be someone who knew he was a believer. In any case, Luis felt he was doomed and that the gods of the cemetery had taken him."

"Well, I can't say its' nonsense any longer." Henry admitted. "I saw how ill he was and I saw his recovery."

Ms K. said quietly, "When one believes – what is this, after all, but the demonic side of Faith?"

Already the memory of the oum'phor was receding, releasing him from its spell so that Henry said almost angrily.

"It goes against everything believable. A man dooming himself to die."

Madam K. said dryly. "Yet, you are witnessing precisely this. You forget that everything that makes a person, a human, is invisible, his thoughts, his emotions, and his soul. You forget that gas is invisible, too, and it can kill. We will all have it in our homes, one day, for lights and to cook with. We use it now, to light the Streets of New Orleans." Finished Katherine wrinkling her pretty nose.

"Okay, the invisible man can kill. Maybe". Said Henry, as he pulled the carriage up in front of Katherine's home. Katherine leaned over and kissed Aunt Alice Goodnight and a Thank You, for her company tonight.

Henry helped Katherine out of the carriage and opened the front door for her.

"It's Nearly Midnight. I left a sign on my door, 'saying that I would be back at twelve and 'Voila' – I am back at twelve. Not the right twelve." She and Ms. Alice laughed, at this little joke.

"I wonder how many patients I lost today." She smiled at Aunt Alice, as she waved Goodbye.

"Good Night, Katherine, my love," said Henry, as he kissed her on her cheek.

Henry drove down the block to Aunt Alice's house next to his and his family.

Good Night Aunt Alice, you are always a love to me on my dates with Katherine. I will see you tomorrow. He kissed Aunt Alice on both cheeks, French Style.

Aunt Alice was his Mothers' sister.

Henry went home and dropped the horse and buggy around the back of the house for Kent to take care of.

"Thank you Kent." Said Henry as he handed him a $5.00 Gold piece.

"Thank you, Mr. Henry and Good Night Sir." Replied Kent

Henry went into the kitchen looking for a plate of food. He knew Ms Bessie would have left him in the oven and a glass of wine to go with his Rosary. He had a lot to pray about tonight.

Good Night Dear Friends.

Chapter Seven

"MS. K. AND LOUISA"

Bailey, Ethel M.T.

Henry's, Ms K., as he called her, was a beauty, a good Catholic, and Henry's Good Friend.

Katherine lived part of the year in New Orleans to attend Loyola University on St. Charles Avenue. Her family owned 'Moon Glow Plantation" on the Bayou Teche' in New Iberia.

The Plantation is one of the best known homes of Louisiana.

Katherine loved the country. New Orleans was, ok, but as Ms K's Mother, Jane, would say, "full of crazy people." Her Husband, Tom would agree. He was a Lawyer and farmer of New Iberia.

So Katherine could be found in her home on the bayou at "Moon" as she and Louisa', her sister, called it.

Louisa' was Katherine's younger sister, by two years. She and Charlie Boy, as all his friends and family members called him, were 'going out'. Which meant, that they were chaperoned whenever and wherever they went out to with a boy, a young gentleman, another person, friend, cousin, or Aunt would be part of the date with the young unmarried couple.

So was Katherine and Henry, and any other boyfriends, she might go on a date with no matter what kind of date. The occasion could be for dinner, dancing, picnic, whatever, unless it was a family occasion at the home of the family having the party.

Katherine liked gardening with her Mother and her sister, Louisa'. The family enjoyed horse shows and showing off their beautiful horses in the park on the Bayou Teche' Trail.

Katherine's horse is a beautiful Arabian, named Goldie. Louisa's horse is a red stallion, beautiful, and too big for Louisa'. But, please don't mention this to her. Her Dad, Thomas, bought him for her when the horse was a colt; no one knew that he would grow to be soooo big.

His name is Tiger. He is strong. Louisa' named him when she was a little girl.

Katherine and Louisa' went to school in New Orleans. They attended the Catholic School of the Ursuline Convent, taught by the Nuns from France. Henry and his Uncles, his friend Charlie, and other boys and girls attended the Ursuline School. It is the best school in New Orleans. This is where Katherine and Louisa' met Henry and Charlie Boy. It is also where other girls and boys of the French and Spanish Culture in the southern part of Louisiana met, courted and were married.

When Katherine and Louisa' were in school, their parents moved from the New Iberia Plantation to the St. Charles Avenue house in the Garden District of New Orleans. This house was known as the Beauvais House. (Beauvais means 'Beautiful View' in French.) This is their home during the school term and the Mardi Gras' Season.

Ms. Kay's House

The family came into town, as they called New Orleans, on many and varied occasions.

New Iberia was about fifteen miles from New Orleans. Henry and Charlie would send notes by hand to be delivered by one of the workers, who went by horseback to deliver them. They would have a meal and a short rest and bring back the answer to the message.

If it was an emergency, Charlie Boy would ask his father Charles Senior to let him and Henry take a run in the Crazy Goose, the plane from the mill. Charlie and Henry treated the plane as their own means of travel, IF they were able to get permission from Charlie's Father, to borrow it.

Katherine, Henry, and Charlie had graduated from College the year before and the ceremonies were beautiful. The Grand Celebration was held at the Roosevelt Hotel for this momentous occasion.

'The Duke', Duke Ellington, and his Band played for the dance that followed the Graduation and the Celebration from the Thomas house on the Avenue to the Roosevelt Hotel on Canal Street.

Everyone looked grand in the elegant styles of the day. White was the predominate color, with soft yellows, greens and pale blues, dotting the dance floor by the girls.

The men were in black Tie and Tails, always looking their best, with whiter than white shirts and highly-polished black boots.

The music was dreamy and jazzy, as only the Duke knows how to play it. A good time was had by all. The Grads danced the night away.

The next day was spent recuperating from the Graduation and the Dance. Then it was time to open the gifts of the occasion and start the list of names for the Thank You Notes everyone must write.

Katherine and Louisa' decided to rest on the swing with a glass of lemonade before writing the list of Thank You Notes that was sitting on the desk waiting for Katherine.

"Oh, well, it will get done. Somehow." Said Katherine to Louisa' with a laugh.

"Not by me," said Louisa', "my turn is coming soon enough."

"It will come sooner than you think, my friend." Said Katherine. "I'll ask Maurine to help me; she likes to write fancy notes." Maurine was Louisa's' Nannie, who she loved and was kept on with the family maids as the girls grew older.

"Maurine will do it." Smiled Katherine, "She loves that blue headband I got as a present from Aunt Pauline in France".

"Better not let Mama hear you say that." Said Louisa'.

There was one Mardi Gras' ball each season at the Belmonte Hotel, near City Park. This ball was given for the Junior and Senior Classes of Boys and Girls who were in separate schools of the Ursuline Campus. The School planned the Ball and was supported by the parents.

Henry claimed Katherine as his partner when he learned she could follow his every step, no matter how wild, fast, or slowly he danced. Quite a feat.

Louisa' refused to dance with Charlie Boy; she was not going to be responsible to her parents for the antics of Sir Charlie Boy." No way!" said Louisa' to Kathrine.

When Katherine told Henry of this decision of her sister, Henry told Charlie and Charlie changed his tune, to 'A Gentleman,' his Mother was determined he would be and his Father aspired too.

Charlie just wanted to dance with the beautiful, joyful, Louisa'. He would do whatever was necessary. And that was being, 'A Gentlemen,' at all times, was Louisa's stance and conclusion to be her dance partner. Huh.

Sir Charlie Boy, found his place and stayed there. There were too many other boys willing to do the gentlemanly manners for Ms Louisa', not a problem. 'Huh', thought Charlie Boy as Henry laughed up his sleeves at Charlie's coming to 'Heel' for the very-lovely young girl.

As Henry became more and more attached to Katherine, he began to see other rivals he had in his vicinity, not to mention, the town of New Iberia, and New Orleans, for competitors for her hand in Marriage. Not just dating, Henry told himself. But marriage and that was what Henry wanted for himself and Katherine. A Permanent Bond.

Chapter Eight

"MARDI GRAS"
(Rex Parade and Ball)

Bailey, Ethel M.T.

The Crews of Organizations such as Rex, King Backus, and other Mardi Gras' Parade floats, were made up of prominent Louisiana families. "King Rex" was the leading float on Mardi Gras' Day in that parade. Tuesday, called 'Fat Tuesday', This is Mardi Gras' Day in New Orleans. This then marked the beginning of Lent, Ash Wednesday.

Henry and Katherine Kurt, MD., had been friends since they were in Catholic School. Henry went to Holy Cross on Carrolton, Ave. and Katherine went to St. Marys' on Loyola, Ave.

Every once in a while there were occasions for the boys of Holy Cross and the girls of St. Mary's to have Social Teas, Dances, Parties, and they made-up the Crews on the Mardi Gras' floats in the parade, such as Rex. The Catholics went from Mardi Gras' celebrations and balls to Ashes and Penance at the stroke of twelve o'clock mid-night on Fat Tuesday. Lent began for millions of Catholics throughout the World. Lent lasted For Forty Days and Forty Nights. Lent had begun with Ash Wednesday. No more Jubilee celebrations for forty days and forty nights.

LENT IS HERE!!!! So this is the way Henry met his good friend Katherine, years ago, whom he called Ms K.

el Rico entered Henry's bedroom in New Orleans!

"Mr. Henry, your coffee Sir, is getting colder than cold; Sir!" el Rico could not exactly fuss at Henry. But....Sassy could.

"Mr. Henry, I hope you got your night gown on like a gentleman should, because here goes your covers, you know I can't mess with you, since you a little boy"-----Swoosh there goes the covers, Henry had all his clothes on from the night before!

Suit, tie, and all.

"Shut your mouth Mr. Henry! It's undignified to sleep that way, you a Gentleman, Sir"

"Huh, el – I never seen the like. How much you think he drank? He ain't moving a muscle!" Frowned Sassy, at the still sleeping Henry.

"You got me Sassy!" Said el Rico, shaking his head slowly, while checking Henry's pulse, "Is he breathing?" Sassy asked?"

"Huh, yep he's snoring lightly." Said el.

"Knock, knock" said someone at the door.

el Rico opened the door a peep to look into the eyes of Ms. Amy.

"Come in, please Ms. Amy, we can't wake up Mr. Henry this morning!" Said el Rico.

"Well, it isn't any wonder! Charlie is sleeping on the couch; he never made it home, just down the street from us."

"Henry! Mr. Henry! Wake up or I will pour COLD water on you." Said Amy in her 'Don't mess with me, son' voice.

"Sorry Mom, I got this headache, el Rico and Sassy are not helping it." Complained Henry, as he drew the covers over his eyes from the bright sun coming in from the big windows in his room.

"No cold water, please el Rico. Mom, please put my feet on the floor, I can't seem to move them to reach it", said a serious Henry.

Amy cocked her head to el Rico and Sassy, to drag Henry out of the bed manually.

"Well, if this isn't the worse I've ever seen you after a night in the Quarters." Laughed Amy, Sassy, and el Rico.

Cafe du Monde

They could not help themselves.

"That's not funny!" squeaked Henry, finally finding the floor.

"Step this way, I'll help you. Sassy has your bath ready and a fresh cup of hot coffee." Said el Rico as he walked Henry to the bath tub.

Meanwhile, Charlie had requested the help of Jerome to "get himself" down the road to his home on the Avenue.

A different Henry descended the stairs and was only a little wobbly on his feet! After Biscuits and eggs, and more coffee, Henry went to meet Charlie to ride together to where the Mardi Gras' floats were kept in a very large barn on Magazine Street.

The Rex Crew was fresh and ready to start the Mardi Gras' Parade on the Rex floats that were beautiful, fun, and colorful, out of the barn and onto the crowded Magazine Street. The biggest parade of the Season.

The King of Rex and his Queen were already waving, throwing kisses and beautiful beads from the famous Float, with many Floats following a few yards in its wake of people and throws.

The King and Queen of Rex met many friends along the way. They threw dozens of Beads and more kisses to their many Subjects.

The Big Bands were strutin' their 'stuff' and beating the drums all along the Mardi Gras' route of the Rex floats. The Majorettes were dressed for a parade and strutted their white tasseled boots until the girls has blisters. But the smiles on their faces never faded.

Strike up the music! The fun has begun, "COME TO THE MARDI GRAS'!".

Parade Float

The Rex Floats made many stops all along the way of the Mardi Gras' route. The Mayor of the City of New Orleans was the first to be toasted at City Hall by the King of Rex and his Queen. The Mayor's wife was waiting on the big steps to toast the King and the Queen of Rex, too. The Champagne flowed all over the city that day.

The next stop was at the Williams' House on St. Charles Avenue, where the Governor of Louisiana, was watching with his friends, Charlie's parents. The Williams', who were holding Court for their family and friends, on the front porch of the Mansion.

Charlie's House

More Champagne Goblets of the Bubbly Wine was flowing in Royal Toast all over St. Charles Avenue.

More High School Bands were strutting their stuff and playing. Come join the Fun! Come to the Mardi Gras', was the delightful music and magic all over the City.

The Parade ended at City Hall where the King and Queen of Rex ended their Royal Reign over the Mardi Gras' Season of the year.

This afternoon, The Holy Rosary was said at the Williams' House on the porch, on St. Charles Avenue, this evening. Both families were gathered there. Amy's and Charles' and other friends up and down the Avenue. An early evening nap will be enjoyed by all Catholics of New Orleans, and the World, before attending mid-night Mass to receive the Ashes that proclaim 'The Season of Lent' has begun.

The Roosevelt Hotel in New Orleans Louisiana was filling up with people from out of town and out of the country.

There was fine dining at Galatois', Brennen's, Antoine's', The Blue Room, etc., etc.

The River Boats were all decorated for Mardi Gras'. Green and Gold are used all over the City.

You could float down the river on the Paddle Wheel, The President, The Mark Twain,' and others, any day of the week.

There is swimming and fishing in Lake Ponchantrain and you could visit the animals at the Audubon' Zoo where there were picnic areas and tables and all kinds of food booths.

New Orleans is also well known as the 'Antique City of the World', I'm just saying.

The French Quarters is known for the Saint Lewis Cathedral, bordered in front by Jackson Square and the Mississippi River. Cafe' du Mon is located there, also.

Another famous street is Canal Street. Many great stores are located there for shopping, meeting and greeting or just having lunch with family and friends.

A famous store is D.H. Holmes. This store is famous for its top quality merchandise and a famous blind Violin Player, who is dressed in a Tux and Tails most days. He plays Classical Music and has an open violin case for wealthy shoppers, and some not so wealthy, to add tips.

Another feature of D. H. Holmes is a beautiful large clock at the front of the store. It was always a phase you could hear up and down the street from friends making a date to "Meet me under the clock".

As the clock struck five o'clock, the wonderful Violin Player, packed up his violin and went to wait for his chaffered limousine to pull up to the curb and his Chauffer to get out and guide the gentleman with his violin to the car and drive away for the day. Part of the Magical History of the Music of the City of New Orleans, Louisiana.

"I'm just sayin'."

And "Meet me under the clock".

The Parades were over.

King Rex of Mardi Gras', has toasted his Wife and his Queen of Mardi Gras', Katherine Kurt, on the steps of the Cabildo Building on Charters Street.

The King and Queen of Rex then descended from the float by a ladder to the steps of the St. Louis Cathedral in the French Quarters and toasted the Priest, Father Jerry, and The Nuns, who congratulated King Rex and Katherine. Then they had a small service in Thanksgiving for a Happy, Safe, Mardi Gras' Season.

Henry then claimed Katherine along with Louisa' and Charlie.

Then everyone left the Cathedral and went home to rest, eat, and nap, to get ready for the balls that were going to take place at the stroke of nine o'clock in the evening. The dancing and the parties go on until the stroke of Midnight, then the party ends and Lent begins.

The Roosevelt Hotel Lobby was filling up at the stroke of 9:00 o'clock, in the evening of Mardi Gras' Day. That's Mardi Gras' in New Orleans, not over yet!

Henry and Katherine went back to the House on St. Charles Avenue, known as "The Rebel House".

They met Amy and the family there, and the servants who could be spared from Idle Wile' and the other plantations for a few days while they helped the family in New Orleans.

The five Arrington families and friends gathered at this great mansion to take part in the parades all week and Mardi Gras' Day with the King Rex and Katherine, the Queen's Parade as well.

The children were having their dinner on the veranda. They were very hungry, thirsty, and tired. In fact, they were being very quiet.

"They were too tired to carry on." Ms Bessie said. There were twelve children in all.

The younger children would eat and their Nannie's would take them off for a much needed bath, books and Prayers, before they got into bed for a long rest.

Josh, Ben, Madeline, Noah, Bella, and the cousins, who were older than eight years old, could go to the ball, for a while. They would have a bath, a rest, then dress as Pages and Flower Girls for the Ball of Rex.

They were quiet, but very excited. They were all asleep when their heads hit the pillow! Three o'clock, nap time.

Josh, Ben, and the boy cousins, went into Uncle Henry's room where el Rico was waiting for them with their black-velvet suits, white shirts, black vest, and a gold tie and black shoes.

What handsome little Pages they would make.

"Don't start picking on Ben, Josh, you will get in trouble. Be good, honey.

The girls were in long white dresses with hair bows of gold. With their long-shiny blond and black hair, they were beautiful Angels.

Everyone was on the balcony watching the carriages go by on the way to the Ball.

The Roosevelt Hotel was lit up with lanterns, candles, and gas lights covered with glass covers that reflected the lights in the mirrors and shiny floors around the ball room. They made the white flowers gleam that were flowing in every part of the Ball Room and Hotel.

Everything looked gorgeous in the lamp light and the big Harvest moon shinning.

The first dance started with the King and his wife and Henry and Katherine, opening the Ball.

There were punch and cake and sandwiches and everything in between to eat and drink.

There were three bands to play for the Ball. They played in turn and had everyone dancing and tapping their feet in time with the music. The bands played music everyone could dance too.

The band started playing a fast dance tune and Henry and Katherine and Josh led the packed house in the dance.

Where is Josh?' Wondered Amy, just as Henry danced by her and handed her Josh's little hand, as he danced off with Katherine.

"Oh well, life goes on," said Amy to Josh as she walked him to the Veranda, where the fireworks were starting to take place. Josh was amazed and starry-eyed at the display of rockets and firecrackers, as he joined his Sisters, Maddie and Bella, Noah, and all the Cousins.

The fire-works kept going off and lighting up the sky. The bands kept playing and people kept on dancing. The party went on until Midnight.

Then the church bells of the Saint Louis Cathedral and other Catholic Church's around the city were ringing the bells to announce the, 'end of Mardi Gras,' and the beginning of Lent. Ashes, Prayers and Penance had begun. (And so did the clean-up of New Orleans, especially Jackson Square.)

Amy and Charlie took the tired children home to a little supper and milk and then to bed.

Amy said, "Thank you and good night, Charlie. See you in the morning at Mass."

"Good night Ms. Amy. Have a good night, get some rest", said Charlie as he took his leave from Amy.

"I will, Charlie. Thank You, Good Night."

Charlie took the carriage back to Jackson Square to meet Henry, Kathrine, Louisa', and the family at the St. Louis Cathedral for mid-night Mass.

Good Night Sweet Friends.

Chapter Nine

"GONE FISHIN'"

Bailey, Ethel M.T.

"Good Morning Mr. Henry. You are some lazy bone this morning." Smiled Ms Bessie, as she handed Henry his early morning cup of coffee in bed. Henry had a hard time waking up and sitting up in bed to drink his hot cup of coffee. The saucer helped him not to spill coffee all over the quilts and sheets. The first sip of coffee was enough to wake him up to pay attention to Ms Bessie, moving to the high windows and drawing the heavy drapes back across the windows to let the light and sunshine in. The heavy drapes kept the room dark and cool. Let the sunshine in, yes, right in Henry's sleepy eyes.

"Ms. Amy is asking about your plans for the day. We staying in New Orleans for a few more days," asked Ms Bessie.

"Well, Ms Bessie, as soon as I can see and maybe remember just where I am this morning, we can discuss it. Was last night Mardi Gras' at the Roosevelt? Ms Bessie."

"Oh no, Mr. Henry, this morning is not the time for you to lose your memory! I'll tell your Mama she needs to come have another cup of coffee in bed with you this morning, or you might be in big trouble, you gonna make all by yourself. My, My, My," Ms Bessie said, shaking her head, as she fussed over Henry's bed clothes, straightening the covers and picking up the empty coffee cup.

"You, ready to see your Mama this morning? I can tell her on my way downstairs, or in the kitchen where she probable is?'

"Mr. Henry, Mr. Henry, don't you go back to sleep, you got a busy day! I know you don't remember what you did last night, but I do and the whole household does too. My, My, My. Mr. Henry, you sound asleep. This calls for Mo' coffee!"

Ms Bessie gave the sleeping Henry one last look as she shook her head, taking the empty coffee cup with her, for a re-fill.

"Ms Amy, you never goanna' believe this." Said Ms Bessie.

"I probably will, since I know you just went with a cup of coffee to serve Henry in bed. Was he up already? "Asked Amy.

"Up, Up!" said Bessie, "I guess not, he drank his coffee and went back to sleep. That's a first for the old saying 'The early bird, catches the worm,' idea he believes in." Laughed Ms Bessie.

"Bessie, I guess he is tired. He was up early yesterday morning and danced the night away.

"Ms Bessie, please ask Sassy to ask el Rico to wait until we are all in the dining room to surprise Jay as he comes into the room. Hopefully, walking on the crutches el Rico made for him. Oh, and please send Sassy to tell Henry of the surprise for Jay. He and Charlie wouldn't want to miss the "Big Event". Poor Jay had to be 'chair bound' for the Parade and the Mardi Gras' Ball." Said Amy.

"Yes, Ms. Amy, I'll take care of that right away." Said Ms Bessie, as she went off to bring the message to Sassy.

"Please wait Sassy," Asked el Rico." I'll be right back."

El Rico found Ms. Amy in the dining room, setting up the big table with white table clothes. Then they were adding china plates, silverware, and crystal goblets. They had placed bouquets of flowers in every available space throughout the room and hall.

Amy and Ms Bessie were busy decorating the dining room for the big surprise, for Jay's journey to wellness and walking once again.

The Pastry Chef was making some special treats for the family and their guest; for Jay's big day.

Finger food, sandwiches, dips, banana foster, fried bread, and candy, to mention a few.

"Ms. Amy, do you mind if I leave Sassy to sit with Mr. Jay and help him with breakfast and coffee while I go see about Mr. Henry and the boys, to see if they need anything I can help them with?" Asked el Rico.

"Oh, el Rico, thank you so much, my mind is not working today." Replied Amy.

"Would you bring a tray of coffee to the boys when you take Henry's upstairs to their rooms? We always seem to need more help, here in New Orleans, when we are here."

"The Harvesting starts as soon as we return to the farms, so there isn't much time left to be in New Orleans this trip." Said Amy, thinking ahead.

el Rico went to the kitchen to find Sassy, who was making fresh biscuits for Henry and the boys and the children's breakfast.

el Rico interrupted Sassy, as Ms Bessie handed him a fresh cup of coffee and a biscuit.

"Thank you Ms Bessie, I need to talk to Sass. Ms. Amy said it is O.K. for her to help Mr. Jay today, while I work with Mr. Henry and the boys."

"Ms. Amy also asked me to take a coffee tray upstairs to Mr. Henry and the children." el Rico, having his errands accomplished, he headed upstairs with the fresh coffee and biscuits on a big tray for Mr. Henry and the children's morning coffee in bed.

el Rico came toward Henry's door, and what did he hear? It sounded like a tribe of Indians had invaded Henry's bedroom by storm!

el Rico politely knocked softly on the door with his elbow. 'Huh', thought el Rico, 'who can hear a polite knock with all that noise going on in that bedroom?'

el put down the heavy coffee tray on the floor and knocked 'BAM' and 'Bam' on the closed door.

"O. K, O.K., el, come on in. I am so happy to see you. I am in dire need of help!" Said Henry. el pushed himself and the heavy tray into the room full of pillows, quilts, and furniture in disarray, mixed with the bodies of boys in their night gowns, already checking out the tray of hot coffee and biscuit's.

"Food!" Said Ben, as he headed toward the tray of coffee and biscuit's, sugar, cream, and syrup.

"Hold on there, Mr. Wolf! Please tell el Rico, Good Morning, and how about, 'thank you', for bringing this treat to us, Sir?" Said Henry.

"Uncle Henry, this is our 'coffee in bed' tray." Said Josh, in a voice that indicated, 'This is not an un-expected treat for the Arrington Children, who receive this privilege every day of the week.'

"Well, little boy, we have manners in this house and you will act like a gentleman to el Rico, who, by the way, is not required to take any guff off you, young man. Corrected Henry, in his,' I'm not kidding,' voice.

"I am sorry, el Rico, I was just playing with you. I do apologize, Uncle Henry and for Little Ben and Noah, here, too." Said Josh as he smiled at Henry.

Ben and Noah, however were not smiling at Josh.

"Josh, help el Rico with that heavy tray. Boys, please pick up the pillows and quilts and put the chairs back where they belong." Said Henry.

el Rico signaled the boys toward the door, and with his Left hand, he drew their attention to the hall. As they followed his hand and his eyes, they entered the hall and looked as el Rico directed them to look down the long hall toward Peggy and Gloria, who were waiting for them.

They signaled the boys to come to them. They ushered the boys into their bedrooms for coffee and biscuits.

Gloria told Peggy, as she was going down the hall to get the tray from Mr. Henry's room, for the boys to please let them have their coffee and biscuits in Josh's bed, if you don't mind. I think they have been punished enough for one day.

"My, my, poor boys." Groaned Gloria, as she walked down the hall to get the big tray from Henry's room. As she approached the room, she could hear those grown men laughing at the boys' disgrace.' Humph,' though Gloria, those are her boys, from babies in the crib.

Henry was talking to el Rico about the fishing trip to Lake Ponchatrain, or the River, with the boys. He was checking with el, to see if he could help Sassy and Ms Bessie fix a picnic basket with sandwiches, cake, and lemonade for them, the boys, Madeline and Bella, if they wanted to go fishing.

"O.K.," said el Rico, who was not overjoyed with a fishing or hunting trip of any kind, anywhere. He liked the Plantation and surrounding areas. After all, he was a Gentleman's Gentleman. He went to the closet and cabinets to check on any clothes suitable for fishing. Uggg.

"Oh, Mr. Henry," said el Rico, "Ms. Amy, and Bessie are preparing the dining room with white table cloths and napkins, silver, and crystal goblets, for Jays' coming Out Party. I hope the crutches are adequate for him to walk with." Said an anxious el Rico.

"el Rico, I think Jay may need you to help him get used to the crutches, so if you don't mind, I think I better leave you here and I can take Jerome with me and the boys for fishing. He can leave the burning of the sugar cane leaves in the fields of the farm to I.J. and Jimmy, who are going back to the farms this morning to tend to this job."

"We should be there also, around, two, this afternoon. We will hopefully clean the fish we catch at Mr. Jeff's Fish Shop, in the French Quarter, all ready to take to the Farms, in time for supper. Yummm." Said Henry. He could taste that fresh fish already.

Henry sent el Rico to spill the plans concerning Jay's 'walk about' on the new crutches and the 'Fishing Expedition' to entertain the boys, girls, Charlie, and Henry.

The dining room was all ready for dinner to celebrate, when Henry and the children came downstairs of the St. Charles avenue Mansion.

Jerome was all for the fishing trip to the Lake or River. He loved to fish. That was his way of relaxing and having a fish-fry with home-made beer, potato salad, and Rice Pudding for desert. Ms Amy agreed with him.

Charlie walked through the front door and wished everyone a 'Good Morning.'

"What's going on?" He asked as he walked into the Library.

"Why are the dining room doors closed? No dinner being cooked today?" Asked an 'always' hungry Charlie.

"Hi neighbor, Charlie. It's nice being in New Orleans, living on the same street. We can come and go between houses, at will." Said Henry, while shaking hands with Charlie.

"How do you feel after the parties last night?" Asked Charlie.

"I'm O. K." Answered Henry.

"In fact, Jerome and the boys and I are going fishing in Lake Ponchatrain. The boys want to go fishing in the 'Ole Muddy.' The Mississippi River." Smiled Henry.

"So we may go there if the girls aren't coming. You know how they turn up their noses up at the River being so close to the banks and how rough the water is, and the smells." Finished Henry.

"So we may go there if the girls aren't coming with us." Said Henry.

"By the way, el Rico is giving Jay his ' Walking Papers' today. He made Jay a 'fine' pair of crutches for him to travel on.

"We hope, he is well enough to manipulate the rooms and porches of the farm where we are taking him back to with the family, hopefully, he can walk without too much pain on the crutches."

"We know he wants to go home." Said Charlie

"Yes, that's the big thing. He doesn't want to hire any help he would need to go back to his house. He needs a cook and we offered Sassy for a couple of weeks. She is more than willing to go, since that is home to her. Her Mother and Dad and family are there in Franklin. I can't give him el Rico, or Jerome, I don't know what I would do without them. But Uncle Jimmy said that Morris likes town and would like to spend a week or more with Jay until he's well."

"What more can you do?" Asked Charlie.

"I agree with him and then let the Judge handle the town situation when we move him. What choice does he have, in that Quarter?" Said Henry.

"He will be happy, just as soon as he realizes that is the best thing for him, if he wants to be home."

"I agree," said Charlie. "I can fly him and his entourage to the Franklin airport in the 'Gray Goose,' if he wants to fly! Or else he can go by horse and buggy with you and Ms. Amy. I hear you're going shopping for the 'Ladies of the household', for favors rendered." Smiled Charlie.

"Yep, got my list and everything. Want to come?" Asked Henry.

"Sure". Answered Charlie. "We can invite Mama and make a holiday of shopping for the two Mothers of ours."

"By the way, when are we going hunting in Charenton Woods again?" Asked Henry.

"Just say the word, now that Mardi Gras' and all that excitement is over, I can go anytime when I'm not fishing or shopping with you." Laughed Charlie.

el Rico opened the door to Jay's bedroom and held it opened for Jay to make his grand entrance maneuvering the new crutches made just for him. Only Charlie and Henry were in the Hall to see the smile on Jay's face and in his eyes, filled with joy to be on his feet again.

Henry and Charlie applauded Jay and el Rico's success. Everyone else waited quietly in the dining room for Jay's grand-surprise entrance.

Jay walked into the dining room, unsuspecting of the reception he was about to have. He is walking on the crutches, el Rico made for him.

Henry and Charlie clapped Jay on the back as Jay was not able to shake hands with his friends. His hands and feet were all busy, with the great gift!

"Yah, Jay, you made it!" Said Henry, happy for his friend who was on his feet again. It had taken at least three months since Jay knocked on Henry's door needing help, and lots of it, and a safe harbor.

Now today was Jay's big day, with the help of Henry's servant who has made a pair of crutches for him to get around on. Jay would be negotiating the house and soon, the yard.

This miracle was by God, for giving the medical skills Henry has to operate on a shattered knee of a shattered man, falling at his door at dawn one day. The man was at the door before the family was out of bed, in the early dawn. He needed help and a safe harbor.

Henry knew this man, but not in the condition he was in, at Henry's door so early in the morning.

Jay was in such bad condition that Henry did not know him at first; Henry did not recognize his friend. He was so banged up and ripped up by something or someone in this neighborhood of the Arrington family's Plantations. But Who? And Why?

After dinner and desert Henry, Charlie, and the boys, said goodbye to Mom.

Henry asked the girls if they wanted to go fishing while the boys busied themselves with tying their shoes and preparing to go to the barn to get the fishing equipment and hid their faces as they were hoping the girls did not want to go fishing.

"Well," said Madeline, "I do like to fish. I might go. How about you Bella?"

"Maddie, are you forgetting what happened the last time we went fishing with the boys?" Asked Bella.

"Well, I guess I did Annabella. What Happened?" Asked Sweet Madeline.

"Well, first Josh found a frog and the only place he could find to put it, was down your blouse." Bella's beautiful blue eyes were shooting fire in their big brothers' direction.

"Oh, Yeah," frowned Madeline.

"And then," continued Bella, " If that was not enough," (who was one, who never forgot a bad prank), "Ben filled a jar of water, dirty water, and poured it down my hair and all over my dress. Yuk and Yuk." Continued Bella, looking precious, even in her anger.

Henry put up his hand and tried to hide the smile on his face while the boys raced to the barn, to Jerome's side.

"Are we to understand, that you two, 'Do Not' want to go fishing???" Asked a serious looking Henry, as Charlie gave out a big shout of laughter he could no longer hold in.

"You can laugh, but just you wait until you get a frog down your shirt and cold, dirty water all over you, if you want to be treated like that." Fussed Bella, getting the last word on the subject.

"Uncle Charlie, you never laugh at Madeline and I, you take up for us." Frowned Bella, as Madeline shook her head in agreement.

"I know girls, and I am sorry I laughed, but Henry is really funny sometimes." Apologized Uncle Charlie.

"I will fish just for you two to eat all the fish you want to, if I'm lucky enough to catch fish." Said Charlie, with a big smile.

"Thank you, Uncle Charlie," chimed in the girls. "Have fun and catch plenty fish. Not you, Josh and Ben, Noah, you can't" Looking like thunder forming on her pretty face.

"What about me?" Asked Henry.

"We don't know about you yet," said the girls, after a conference in whispers. "We have to pray on it, for you." Laughed the girls as they ran to the front porch to swing and watch them leave.

Jerome had all the fishing equipment ready for the big fishing trip to the banks of the Mississippi River at the foot of Canal Street.

Charlie had gone to the stables on Magazine Street and was waiting with his driver and horse and buggy on the curb by Henry's home, all ready to load the fishing gear and the boys for the much awaited for fishing trip to the banks of the 'Ole' Muddy', The Mississippi River. The best fishing spot in Louisiana.

The boys were so excited, they almost fell out of the buggy before it stopped.

Henry and Charlie could only laugh out loud; it reminded them so much of themselves as boys, at that age. Same thing happened to them.

Strong memories were with them on account of these young boys. Man, were they glad to have them along for fishing in the river.

"Look, Uncle Henry," said Ben. "A red bird sitting on that branch hanging over the water, right there."

"Shush." Said Henry, "He is very beautiful and he caught a worm on the wet bank. I bet he will bring it to his nest to feed his mate and the little red birds."

"Yes, watch boys. There he goes, let's see if we can follow him to his nest." They were very sneaky when it comes to following them to the location of their nest. "Yep, there he goes into the hanging branches of that old Oak tree. Nobody can see him and the nest in all that bushy growth."

"Still, was nice to see him, though," said Ben. Who always had a happy ending for any experience.

Charlie and Ben Fishing

"Yep," said Charlie, "Look Ben, you got a bite. Quiet or we will scare him away." Whispered Charlie. "Pull up sharp to set the hook, yes, just like that. Now, pull your pole up and backward and we will snag him with the net."

"I don't know who is the most excited, you Charlie, or the boys." Said Henry, teasing Charlie.

"No contest." Answered Charlie, "it is ME! I love fishing and being with you and the boys."

Ben cast his line back into the dark waters of the Ole' Muddy, as the Mississippi River was called in Louisiana. 'Come on fish, bite,' thought Ben, 'just one fish is not going to feed too many people. I need lots of fish and crabs.' There goes one now, watching a big blue claw crab crawling along the edge of the river, not quiet out of the river, but just along the edge of the water.

Josh was busy as a bee trying to get a bite on his line before Ben caught another fish.

"Look Uncle Henry," said Josh "another red bird. He has something in his beak. Must be a bug for the little peeps in the nest."

"I see it Josh, it has a worm it's bringing to the nest of little peeps for lunch, and they have their mouths open all the time waiting for the Mother bird to drop food into it." Laughed Henry.

'Yuk,' thought Josh, 'I wouldn't open my mouth for any ole' worm or any food the peeps eat. Yuk and Yuk.' Josh couldn't express enough words as to just how bad this sounded to him.

'The river was calm today, considering the breeze that was blowing up stream.' Thought Henry.

"We are not catching anything," He said as he lay back on an old log "except for Ben here".

"Bite, Bite," said Noah as he cast his fishing line out into the still waters of the river. "Fish or Crab, I don't care." Said Noah.

A Mosquito Hawk flew close to the tip of Josh's nose, he looked cross-eyed at the beautiful bug and thought, "Come here bug, you're pretty enough to use for bait on my little hook for a big Red Fish, uh-huh, uh-huh, smarty cat, fly away over the water, the big fish will jump up in the air and catch you and eat you in one bite."

Mosquito Hawk

"Look, Look!" shouted Charlie, 'That big Red Fish jumped into the air and caught that Mosquito Hawk! He was flying to close to the water, Josh. I never saw that before in my life! How 'bout you Henry?"

"Nope never did. I've heard fellows talking about it happening, but not me." Said Henry shaking his head.

Charlie slapped his knees with his hands with great gusto at the sight of nature they had all witnessed.

Noah, Josh, and Ben, looked at each other and Josh said, "Well Ben, we didn't have to be as old as Uncle Henry and Mr. Charlie to see such a sight on the Ole' Muddy." They laughed.

"Ha." said Josh, "Just as I thought it would happen." He laughed at the funny sight.

"Aw, go on," laughed Ben and Charlie and Uncle Henry, "you never in this world thought of that happening".

"Yes, I just did," complained Josh, "you never believe me".

"That's because you think of it after it happens Josh. We don't fall for that kind of imagination."

"But its' true!" Frowned Josh, his blue eyes flashing.

"We believe you think that way, so we'll say – O.K. it happened, just as you thought it would." Grinned Uncle Henry. Ben was shaking his head to confirm Uncle Henry's baloney!

"Thanks, Uncle Henry and Ben, I knew you would believe me!" Grinned Josh.

"Here boys, have a sandwich and a cup of lemonade." said Henry.

"Yes, Sir," said the boys at once. They sat down on the grass under the oak trees to eat.

Josh

They fed the crumbs to the birds and squirrels to, who ever got there first. Usually the wily squirrels beat every other animal to food!

"Any Luck?" asked Uncle Henry, eyeing the fishing lines the boys were holding patiently over the calm water of the river.

"Not yet." Said Ben. "No fish for supper tonight". He groaned. Josh looking side-ways at Ben patiently waiting for a bite on his line.

"Maybe there will be," grinned Henry "Look across the river. Who's boat do you suppose that is? I bet they have a lot of fish for supper."

"Noc, Noc Knoc'!" Shouted the boys as the Captain of the boat took off his hat to wave to his Kin Folks, across the water.

"Hello, Hello, Noc Knoc', any luck today?" We are flat, none, no fishing luck today." Shouted Henry.

"The fish are jumping into my boat, all day. Plenty fish for everyone," Laughed Uncle Gustave.

"Of course, I catch, you clean!" Winked Gustave, as he maneuvered his flat bottom boat to the North Shore of the River.

"Of course," smiled Henry, Charlie, and the boys.

"As long as we get a fried fish supper like only Ms Bessie can cook fish and don't forget the potatoes salad," said Josh, Noah, and Ben, all together laughing.

Noc Knoc' stepped off the boat as Henry held onto the rope to steady the fishing boat as it bobbed up and down on the water

"Henry, you, Charlie, and the boys, pick your fish out of my catch while I go to the towns' wharf to deliver my catch to the Market. You can clean your fish there. Then I'll be by your house in a little while for a glass of your fine wine and a little dinner of fresh fish and all Ms Bessie's fine dishes that go with it." Chuckled Uncle Gus as Henry, Charlie and the boys fished the easy way – off the boat of Noc Knoc'.

Boats

"Ms. Amy and Ms Bessie walked over to the Cistern where Henry, Charlie and the boys were busy working on 'Something.'

"Oh, no," chanted the ladies at the same time! "Could it really be fish this time?" And what a beautiful catch, they had brought home.

Ms Bessie hurried her steps to the work bench and the pan of clean water, Henry, Charlie and the boys were quickly filling up with big white fish.

"Be careful Henry," Ms Bessie said, "you must filet the fish just so, to fry crisp." Amy said eyeing the fresh, beautiful full basin of fish.

"I know, I know, Mama, we are taking great care to do it just right. We want a great fish fry."

"Ms Bessie, tell us how you want them and we will carry out your orders. You're the cook, you know, and we know too."

Henry was ready to turn over the cleaned and cut up fish to Ms Bessie. Henry and Charlie wanted a bath, clean clothes, and a glass of red wine while they waited for Noc Knoc' to join them on the front porch, rocking while waiting for Ms Bessie and Sassy to call them to Supper.

The boys, Josh, Noah, and Ben, were sleeping on the day beds in the big hall upstairs. They were worn out with catching so much fish. (Or trying to catch all that fish, Whew.)

"Where are Noah and Josh?" Asked Charlie when he saw Jerome coming in for supper with the family.

"The boys are bushed," said Henry, "They are having a nap after their baths that took the rest of their energy out of them. Mama said she was going to wake them up, when Uncle Gustave gets here."

"Good evening, Gentlemen. I hear you had quite a catch on the River today." Smiled Jerome as he sat on the swing with Amy.

"Well you got part of it right. We had the worst luck today, as far as fishing goes, the only fisherman amongst us was, Ben, he caught the first, last, and only fish of the day. He was so proud." Said the fisherman of the Arrington family, who always came home with the most fish.

"Bong, Bong, Bong," said the plantation bell from the front yard. This was a most popular time for the big bell to ring. In the evening. It rang out the end of the day. All farm work was done and supper was ready. Time to relax.

Just as Uncle Gustave's horse rounded the fence of the lawn and one of the stable boys went to get the horse to take him into the barn.

Ms Bessie came out to the porch to call the family into the dining room for the fish-fried supper with potatoes salad, french bread, Iced tea and dessert.

Josh, Noah, Ben, Madeline, and Bella were right on time for the Meal Prayer.

The fried-fish dinner was delicious!

After the meal was over, the family went back to the porch to talk, rock, and swing their heavy meal into an easy feeling.

Uncle Gustave called for his horse and rode down his road home; near Uncle Jimmy's Farm.

Jerome said 'Goodnight' to the family and left for his home.

The family, and Uncle Charlie, reached for their Rosary' to Recite.

They thanked God for a wonderful, safe day, and went to bed.

Goodnight Family and Friends.

Chapter Ten

"THE HARVEST"

Bailey, Ethel M.T.

The Harvest

RA-TA-TAT, RA-TA-TAT, RA-TAT-TAT a - VERY – LOUD Wood Pecker was piercing the early morning- Quiet, at Day break. (They don't care!)

"WHAT is he doing?" Ben asked, the gray dawn coming through his windows. "That bird is so loud."

Ben's door opened gently, not to wake up Ben, just in case he was still sleeping with all that noise going on outside his window.

Josh tip-toed into Ben's room, his toes sinking into the thick velvety carpet towards Ben's bed.

"Hey Josh, what you doing in here," asked Ben, not too quietly.

"Shush, big mouth, I just wanted to see if you were up this morning!" Whispered Josh as he ran to shut the door before one of the Nannie's found him missing from his room so early in the morning.

"What woke you up so early, Ben?" Asked Josh.

"Josh, you the one on the move so early, what woke you up?" Asked Ben as he frowned at Josh.

"That stupid bird, that's what woke me up," whispered Josh. "Is that what woke you up?"

"Yes," said Ben, "you better watch your talk; we not allowed to use the 'stupid' word, no time and nowhere," said Ben to Josh.

I know, Ben, sorry. Glad the Nannie's didn't hear me, anyway, that loud bird out there is a Woodpecker." Said Josh.

"What's he so loud about, so early this morning, anyway?" Asked Ben.

"Well Ben, he's pecking a hole in that tree, looking for bugs that live in the tree," said Josh.

"UGGG," said Ben, "that ruined my breakfast, for sure."

Josh laughed as Ben made a sour face about the Woodpecker.

"I can tell you, that bird will not ruin my breakfast." Said Josh,

The door opened and in came Gloria carrying a tray of -- you guessed it -- two hot cups of fresh coffee and hot biscuits. The biscuits were dripping with country butter. There was also heavy cream and sugar for the hot fresh coffee. The silver ware was wrapped in a white linen napkins.

"Well, there you are Josh. Ms. Amy said I could find you in Ben's room if you were missing from your room early in the morning, and sure 'nuff, here you are." Smiled Gloria.

"She said you would crawl in bed with Ben or Mr. Henry, but he doesn't want anyone to wake him up, unless they had his hot coffee on a tray. He trained el Rico and Ms. Amy well that Mr. Henry", laughed Gloria, as she placed the coffee tray on the little tea table she placed between the two boys.

el Rico was entering Mr. Henry's room with his tray, as Gloria came down the long hall laughing to herself at the two boys she had just left with their 'early morning coffee' she had just served them. They were talking a mile a minute about the noisy Woodpecker outside their windows and eating and drinking coffee as fast as they could. They were starving.

el Rico came into Henry's room, not thinking he would have to wake him up. Usually Mr. Henry was awake. Henry would just be dozing while waiting for el Rico to bring in his coffee and biscuits.

"Good Morning, Mr. Henry," said el Rico as he entered the bedroom.

"Ummm-m," groaned Henry. 'He was not ready to wake up just yet.' thought el Rico. He put the coffee tray down on the table next to Henry's bed, just close enough for him to smell the fresh coffee and not close enough for him to spill it.

el Rico went over to the big, high, wide windows at the foot of Henry's bed and pulled back the heavy dark drapes to let in the early morning daylight of a new dawn.

"Morning, el, what time is it?" Asked Henry. As he yawned and yawned himself awake.

"What is that smell?" Asked Henry, watching el Rico set up the small tea table in place for his coffee and biscuit tray.

"They burning the sugar cane leaves this morning, Mr. Henry, for the Harvest." Replied el Rico.

"What!?" Yelled Henry, looking at el Rico.

"Yes Sir, Mr. Henry, you gave orders to start the sugar cane leaves burning on Idle Wile', early this morning. And they are doing just that." Answered el Rico, as he turned around to pick up a napkin from the floor, so Henry could not see the smile on his face. 'Gotcha,' thought el Rico, after all these years. He picked up the napkin and faced Henry's bed. el Rico was not being disrespectful toward Henry; it was a game they started many years ago. el Rico trying to catch the human side of his boss, Mr. Henry, and Henry taking the pains and the joy to beat his servant and friend at the game.

'Oh well,' thought Henry, 'Had to happen one day, today be the day.' He said to himself. "el Rico, close those window and ring the bell and tell Ms Bessie and the Nannies to close all the window and doors of the house. Quickly!" Said Henry.

"We did, Mr. Henry, as soon as everything and everyone were in place. Ms. Amy and your Uncles are all here to watch the burning and they have a lot of water on hand in case it's needed to stop any small flare-ups." Said el Rico, facing the windows, making sure they were not open. He closed the one he had just opened to wake up Henry with the smell.

el Rico had taken out Henry's farm clothes so he could be outside with the men to make sure the men, animals, and property and "The Harvest" was safe.

Henry dressed, drank his coffee and ran down-stairs. He jumped over the boys, who just showed up on the curve of the stair. Henry hadn't seen them in his path to the sugar cane fields, where he was headed at break-neck speed. Still, he managed to avoid sending them rolling down the stairs.

Henry, slowed down in the back hall by the door of the kitchen where the Uncles and Mama were having breakfast.

"Where are the boys, Henry?" Asked Amy.

"I left them rolling down the stairs on my way down-stairs. No, No, Mama, they should be here now. Yep, there they are. Where are the girls? Getting out of the hard work we have today?" Laughed Henry, as he waited for Mama's sharp reply defending her girls.

"Sorry Mama, I was just wondering where they were this morning. I don't want them working on the burn or any other field work either." Apologized Henry.

"Henry, once more, girls and women do not work in the fields! That's mens work, whether some men agree or not. That does not happen here!" Said an annoyed Amy.

"Further Henry, the girls and women are at Uncle I.J.'s plantation, baking and making salads and sandwiches for the workers and families that are hard at work with the burn." Said Amy.

"Thanks, Mom. I couldn't have put it better myself. I was just wondering where they were, and said the wrong thing. I'm sorry." Said Henry.

"That's alright, Henry, I'm just a little worried every time we have to burn fields of sugar cane leaves from the stalks of cane. So many things can happen."

"So much work and so dirty, for everyone. Thank God, the Bayou and the River are close by to wash the smoky, dirty clothes and dirtier workers in. Everyone goes swimming to get most of the smoke and dirt from their bodies and clothes. Octagon Soap helps a lot to scrub clothes and people clean." Said Amy with Ms Bessie agreeing with her.

"We need lots of strong soap." agreed Ms Bessie, with Sassy agreeing with her.

These ladies knew 'Soap,' they made lots of it every year.

Six days had passed since the first day of the 'Burn' of the sugar cane leaves in the fields of the plantations.

The fields were left alone for a few days to allow the burned cane to cool down, then the workers went to the first field and started the clean-up process. The rest of the fields were cleaned in turn as each field cooled down.

Soon all the fields were cleaned of burned leaves and other trash. This dirty, smelly trash was piled-up at the edge of each field to be picked up by Oxen-pulled carts and brought to the forest to deep pits dug for disposal.

The field hands were dead tired and their lungs were full of smoke from the fires. This is the last day of the cleanup of the sugar cane stalks and fields. Henry gave the field hands, and any other Harvest worker, three days off to rest, and to be treated for the smoke that settled in their lungs. Henry never left Idle Wile' at this time of year. Trappers, hunters, or lumber men riding the logs down the Red River, had to be taken to Henry for treatment.

Henry and Charlie have been working together for the burning of the sugar cane leaves, with the men in the field, ever since they were young boys. They were skilled in using a cane knife and driving cane wagons, with the power of Oxen to pull the loaded wagons. They drove the wagons into the forest where there were big, deep pits to dump the burned leaves into. These pits had been dug many years ago by Henry's Father and Grandfather. The leaves took all year to turn into rich fertilizer for the crop plantings and the rose gardens which were to be found by the library's double-french doors on the west side of the house.

Amy spends any spare time she has during the day to rest with a cup of coffee and a time to pray her Rosary in the Rose Garden. Family and friends drop by to visit a while when they have time. The usual time for these visits is nine o'clock in the morning. A special time to take a break and pray with Amy and the girls and whoever shows up with a Rosary, in a beautiful, restful place.

The sugar cane crop was planted each year on eighteen hundred Arpan's (Acres) of land. The fields were planted and harvested by the five Arrington families and their workers.

Other plants such as lettuce, tomatoes, peppers, other vegetables, and fruit trees are grown in the kitchen garden. These vegetables are used every day for cooking and for making fruit preserves.

The eight hundred acres are cultivated and planted with vegetables to produces big crops. These are the vegetable crops for the Arrington's, their workers, and for sale at the local stores.

The livestock, poultry, dairy cows, and hogs, are also grown to benefit the same people. Horses and all farm animals are also part of the farm and do their share of work and receive the best of care.

The sugar cane crop is the most work intensive crop to plant and to harvest. When the plants mature, the leaves on the stalks are burned off. After the stalks of cane cool down, the cleaning of the fields and the harvesting of juice from the cane begins.

The stalks of cane are cut into pieces and then crushed to obtain the sweet juice it contains. Then the juice is boiled into sugar.

The work involved in the process of taking the sugar cane stalks to the point where they are ready to be crushed and boiled in copper-lined vats is work intensive and demanding. Not to mention, hot, dirty, and dangerous.

Boiling the juice of the cane into sugar is a giant undertaking on its own.

Ms Bessie was bustling about; she loved this time of year. However, it was a hot, dirty, and a tiringly hard job.

The Harvest Time came around in the fall of the year. October, to be exact.

Ms. Amy came into the area known as the 'Compound', which was a large area occupied with three big water cisterns that caught the rain fall to provide water for the house and farm. The water was used for drinking, making lemonade, coffee, root beer, cooking, bathing, and drinking water for family and the animals. The laundry and water for the gardens and fields were brought from the bayou and the river by using the water cart.

As Amy reached the edge of the compound, she saw that Bessie was there ahead of her. This was of no surprise to Amy.

"Hello, Ms Bessie, how are you today?" Asked Amy

"I'm fine, Ms. Amy, are you well?" Replied Ms Bessie.

"I am well, Ms Bessie and ready to get on with the 'crushing' of the sugar cane stalks. Jerome said they had been cleaned of burned leaves and were ready to be cut into sections for the crushing machine."

"Thank God, we have that machine to extract the juice from the stalks of cane." Said Amy, thinking of all the work this process involves, with or without the machine. 'With' was much better'

"Henry's watching for Lil' Wolf, the Braves and Maidens of the Chitimacha Tribe, to come and help us with this big Job." Said Amy as she reached Ms Bessie, in a few steps.

"They should be here soon."

"Is the Compound area ready to be cleaned, Ms Bessie"? Asked Amy.

"Yes, Ms. Amy, we just have to sweep the ground, get rid of the trash, and cover the entire area with the new canvas." Said a smiling Bessie.

Big vats were lined with copper and they were used to boil the cane juice to make sugar. The making of sugar from the juice of the sugar cane is a long and tiring process. The outcome makes sugar the most valuable "cash" crop in Louisiana.

The crops that are sold in the town markets are called the "CASH" crops. There are other uses for cash, one is the purchase of equipment. The cash is mainly used to pay the servants of the large houses, the field hands, and all other workers on the farms.

Cash is also needed to purchase furniture, rugs, stoves, saddles, rope, shoes, hats, material, and all other needed Items, not produced on the farms.

Now the hardest and most dangerous job of the sugar cane production has to be the sugar cane process known as 'Crushing' of the burnt, cooled, sugar cane stalks.'

Ms Bessie had left Sassy and the kitchen maids in charge of the kitchen. Yes, the cooking for two-hundred plus family, friends, and workers of the harvest. Pitchers of lemonade, water, root beer, are made in big buckets and cooled in the ice cellar.

Gloria and Sue were in charge of the children. All of them, the lucky number of thirteen (13) in all, babies' included. With the help of the other six Nannies from the other four Arrington families; who would also help in the kitchen and vegetable gardens, during nap time for the children.

Ms Bessie was in charge of everything else that had to do with feeding, cleaning, setting up eight-foot wooden tables found in the barn. Directing any of the men she could corral to help and fussing about in general.

Sassy started making roux on the giant iron pot belly stove in the cook house, about six feet from the main house. The purpose of having a cooking house, apart from the main house, is not to burn down the whole plantation in case of fire breaking out while cooking and baking.

The servants were washing vegetables, onions, garlic, and sweet peppers for a big stew. A five-gallon pot of rice was started and three giant pots of red beans were put on to boil.

Ms Bessie started the men in her charge, setting up tables and benches under the giant oak trees in the back yard. They also placed blankets on the ground for the children to play and to eat on.

Next on Ms Bessie's agenda was cleaning and setting up the Compound with clean canvas sheets.

The Compound area was being prepared for pressing the juice from the stalks of sugar cane into big copper vats to boil into grains of sugar. Willow tree branches were used to sweep the Compound of all debris.

After the Compound was cleaned, a new canvas blanket was used to cover the dirt floor of the Compound. The blanket were laid on the ground under the kettles and spread over the hard dirt floor of the Compound.

The Chitimacha Tribe of Charenton, Louisiana, is 'Best Friends' of Henry and the Arrington family. Each year at "Harvest" time, the Chitimacha Tribe and its Braves and Maidens come to the Compound to help the Arrington Family, and especially Henry, with the Harvest.

In return, Lil' Wolf, his father 'The Chief', and the Tribe, receive a year's supply of sugar, and vegetables, and fruits. Yummmm! And the everlasting friendship and thankfulness of Henry, Amy, and the Arrington families and workers.

The compound area was in front of the largest field of sugar cane. The big water cisterns are located here. The Compound is used only for pressing the cane juice into the big heavy brass kettles that are used for boiling the sweet juice until it turns into grains of sugar when dried.

No children were allowed in the Compound once the area was cleaned and in use for the crushing of the cane. This is a very dangerous area once the crushing of the cane starts. Also, the compound had to be kept clean, for the process of making sugar.

Lil' Wolf and his warriors were in charge of the crushing of the cane for the Juice. Their leather clothes were very beautiful, mostly white or cream and decorated with many beads, tassels, and fringe. Their Maidens, who were wearing fresh flowers in their flowing black hair, were riding behind each one of them.

Little Wolf and his young Warriors came to the outer edges of the compound with much dignity and self-possession. The Chitimacha Warriors were at Idle Wile' Plantation to press the juice from the burned, hard, sugar cane stalks.

Lil' Wolf, who was full of pomp and circumstance and was riding with the staff of many colored feathers flying above him, came into the clearing of the lawn area from the forest coolness.

Henry, Charlie, and Amy were on hand to greet Lil' Wolf and his Tribe. The children, not wanting to be left out of this experience and happy times, were sitting quietly on the front porch where they would not miss a thing, they hoped.

Lil' Wolf, always the performer, gave a kick to his Creole Pony and the pony bowed as he bended one knee to the ground.

"Welcome, good friends." Said Henry.

"Thank you, good friend, Henry, Charlie, and Mama." Answered Lil' Wolf.

Lil' Wolf, waved his arms toward the company of Braves and Maidens that accompanied him for the Harvest.

Henry, thanked Lil' Wolf and walked him to the compound cleaned by Bessie and helpers. This is the area for the crushing of the sugar cane into juice and pulp; the job Lil' Wolf, his Braves, and Maidens chose to do. Having so much man power to crank the wooden handle that turns the wheel of the big cane crusher makes the job move along at a steady pace.

These are the most efficient workers ever known to accomplish this job in the shortest measure of time.

Lil' Wolf and his tribe followed Henry, Charlie, and Amy to the Compound which had been swept and cleaned of trash and covered with canvas blankets.

The Uncles had prepared the tubs of water for the washing of the feet of whoever were going to work in the Compound, namely the Chitimacha Tribe, Lil Wolf', and Jerome.

Jerome's feet had been washed, so he walked bare-footed on the clean canvas.

Lil' Wolf and each of his Warriors sat on a chair. The Maidens sat in front of the many tubs filled with clean water to wash their Warriors feet, who then could follow Jerome and Lil' Wolf to the crushers across the canvas covering the dirt floor. The big cisterns were close at hand to change the water as needed by the Maidens.

The Maidens, then washed each other's feet with many giggles from the tickles.

All set, all ready.

Lil' Wolf and the Braves followed a bare-footed, Jerome with the Maidens following Lil' Wolf, all bare-footed. Not a condition new to them.

Ms Bessie went to collect several giant trays of sandwiches and pitchers of root beer and water for the hard working men and women in the compound crushing cane and boiling juice into sugar.

Root beer was Lil' Wolf and his people's favorite white mans' drink.

The Uncles were in charge of each section and process of the sugar cane harvesting of the day. The boiling and cooling of the syrup of the cane had to be closely watched for the successful outcome of each day. The completion of the process had to be successful at every step. The next step of sugar making is the storing of the sugar.

The finished product of sugar was stored in clean, new, barrels, lined with pillow cases and covered with a wooden top to keep out the dampness, any dust, and or pest.

One of the problems Henry has, during this time, is his concern for the responsibility as the Doctor of the region, the swamp, forest, and the near-by towns, included.

Charlie and el Rico have the responsibility of being by Henry's side in case of an emergency. You will see how this works, in a few minutes. Read on po-lease.

Henry and Charlie were black as coal from collecting the burned leaves and debris, a big burned mess.

Charlie was handling the Ox that was pulling the wagon back from the forest 'pits of darkness,' as they called the pits of burned leaves and other trash.

"Charlie, pull-up to the outer lawn area and stop." Said Henry, watching a bunch of men on the front porch and steps.

"Thank God." murmured Charlie, as he pulled backwards on the ropes that were tied to the Oxen's mouth piece. His body left the seat of the wagon as he strained to stop the beast before it trampled the beautiful green lawn and yards of Day Lilies and Crepe Myrtle trees that lined the drive on the way to the front of the Plantation.

"WOAH, WOAH, S T O P, HARD HEAD!" Yelled Charlie at the Ox.

"Well, Charlie, are you able to stop one poor Ox in its tracks? Do you need my help?"

"Shut up, Henry, you could have given me a little more warning, that you were ready for a break. Sir." answered Charlie, as he was always ready for Henry's smart mouth on occasions when they were both tired, irritable, dirty, hungry, thirsty, and just darn 'Mean' feeling.

'Enough is enough.' thought Charlie, not a bit apologetic. 'HuH!!!'

"Charlie, stop the dumb Ox, man, I hate it when you make me yell at you. There are men on the porch; I think they came from the logging enterprise your Dad owns. They may need help._Someone could be hurt." Said Henry, ready to jump off the high seat of the wagon.

"Wait, wait, Henry, Just give me a hand and I can stop this old hard head, Ox. I have been mauling my hands on this rope, it's killing me. Help me stop him." Shouted Charlie.

Henry jumped on the Oxen's broad, dirty, scratchy back and pulled on the rope to his mouth that had an iron bit in it to hold the rope's bridle and to control him. (Not so much!!).

All the men on the porch turned around when they heard Charlie's colorful language addressing Henry who looked like a circus acrobat on the back of the Ox.

That stopped him. He was one bad, mad Ox. Henry jumped off the animal's back, in double time.

Henry helped Charlie down from the wagon seat and they ran to the porch full of strangers and friends, alike.

"What is the matter," Yelled Henry, before he reached the steps to the porch.

"Henry, Mr. Charlie had us bring Simon to you because he jabbed a gig into his foot; he was trying to grab a run away log that had gotten loose from the ropes holding them togEther. Looks real bad and hurts worse, I imagine." Said Elroy Jackson.

Simon was sitting on the swing with his leg on a pillow, blood streaming everywhere. But, Ms Bessie had given him and all the men, about three in number, glasses of lemonade.

"Bless you Ms Bessie." said Henry, as she handed he and Charlie each a big glass as well.

"Gentlemen, let's get him inside on the library couch where he can be comfortable and where my Medical bag is," said Henry, as Charlie lifted the pillow and the hurt foot in both hands, while the other men picked up Simon to carry him inside where Ms Bessie was holding the double doors open to fit them all in.

Gloria and Sassy heard the commotion on the front porch just in time to hear Henry say:

"Carry him into the Library and put him on the couch." 'Oh No,' thought Gloria while Sassy led the way to the linen cupboard and they got sheets and blankets to make up the library couch for another patient.

Sassy and Gloria did not say a word to each other, there was no time.

They reached the library just as Jerome came into the room to see if he was needed.

"Yes, indeed," said Gloria and Sassy. Plantation women never turned down the offer of a man's help.

Jerome opened the library doors to the great hallway. Then he moved the couch closer to the lamps while Sassy and Gloria unfolded the sheets and made up the couch with a set of new white ones. Then the blankets were ready to be put there also. Jerome had unfolded them while waiting for Sassy and Gloria to put on clean pillow cases over the pillows of the couch.

Just as the couch was ready and Jerome had grabbed Henry's black bag from the desk, Henry and the men carried Simon into the library.

Henry tilted his head toward Jerome, Sassy, and Gloria in appreciation of their timely good work. Charlie had just come back in after a few minutes from washing up to help Henry with the surgery. el Rico was with him.

el Rico had been helping with the mid-day meal being carried by shifts of cooks, family, and friends, to under the giant oak trees for about two-hundred hungry, tired workers.

Jerome handed Henry his medical bag and two large towels, and another wet one to wash his hands and arms with. One had soap on it. Then he handed Henry a small dram of whiskey, Henry drank a couple of big swallows, Jerome filled the glass again and motioned for Henry to wash his hands with that whiskey. Hmmmmmm.

"Please ask one of the Uncles to send for Morris, Mr. Charlie's chauffer, to come to the house. He will be needed to pick up Simon to take him home after the surgery. His wife and family can give him the care he will need."

"We are ready to start the surgery." Said Henry.

"Thank you, Jerome, please ask Sassy and Gloria to make a lot of sandwiches and coffee for all of us. We are all hungry, thirsty, and dirty."

"Please tell Mama where we are and have Marshal take the Ox wagon to the cane field so someone else can take care of the burnt leaves, it's almost finished, it just needs one more load or maybe someone has done it." Said Henry, as he washed his face, hands, and arms, again and poured the glass of whiskey over his hands and arms, as el Rico watched the process.

Henry made the Sign of the Cross, asking for the help of Jesus, to save this young man, who had bled so much and had enough pain to boot. The shank of the pole was sticking up from Simon's bleeding foot. The pole with its vicious hook and curved balancing post was never easy on the eye, except to spear a log to roll it in line with the other logs. Men walked on the logs headed down the swift Red Rivers' water. That was a hard job, an almost impossible one.

Sure enough, el Rico came into the room with a Dram of Whiskey that was well received by the patient. He also had the little vial of Ether and clean, folded rags to administer it.

Simon grinned from ear to ear, even though the pain was still in his eyes, he tipped the dram of whiskey to Henry, who laughed and bowed to him. Henry used a little whiskey to rinse his hands to the elbows, to sanitize them again, for the surgery. They would all get a dram after the surgery.

el Rico lowered the rag of Ether below Simon's pain-filled eyes, as he closed them tight; the breath of Ether he inhaled started its magic. Simon looked forward to the Ether to wipe away the pain and the anxiety of the surgery.

As soon as Henry was sure Simon was unconscious, he took the saw that Jerome had brought in from the barn, just in case Henry needed it. Charlie was holding Simon down on the couch, just in case he could hear the sawing, that must be used to cut the pole from the hook.

The first part of the surgery was finished without a hitch. Simon had not moved as Henry sawed off the pole from the hook in his foot. Henry looked at the spear in Simon's foot. "Humph," said Henry. The spear was between the big toe and the second toe. 'Not a pretty site.' thought Henry as he gathered the instruments from el Rico's hand, to start the first cut on the injury.

Henry decided to cut between the two toes, to cut out the iron hook and spear head. He asked Charlie what he thought about this procedure. Charlie agreed after asking el Rico for his opinion, too. They both agreed.

"el Rico, please go get more clean rags because the knife will cause more bleeding. Also get a couple of towels, and please ask Amy which ones to take, because they are going home with Simon, thanks." Said Henry as a bead of cold sweat appeared on his forward.

He had to watch out for the vital arteries, nerves, blood vessels, small bones, and God knows what else in Simon's foot, that could go wrong, or he may be crippled for life.

'Damn, I should have paid more attention to Dr. Carlton, and to his instructions. I wrote them down to help me in such a surgery, but, I had no time to study them before Simon needed me.' Thought Henry as he took great pains to know just where the knife was cutting.

Henry made the cut between the two toes and cut around the hook and spear head. He then removed the iron hook and spear head. More blood and a groan from Simon. Henry nodded to el Rico for more Ether. el Rico was ready with more clean towels, too.

Henry threaded his needle with cat-gut and he and Charlie wiped the wound several times to stop the blood flowing from it.

"el Rico, please hold the toes togEther for me to stitch the wound. Please try to hold them with a small hand towel. I think I can sew it up better." said Henry.

"Charlie, it just occurred to me, concerning your Father. I hope you agree with me. I think, maybe you could write him a note, telling him what has happened and invite him to come here while Simon is resting, after the surgery. I think he would like to know firsthand just what happened to one of his employees and friend. What do you think of that Idea?" asked Henry as he took another stitch to close the wound.

"It's a fine idea Henry; I think I will write it now, on your finest stationary." Replied Charlie boy.

"Well, be sure and use the best envelope too," said Henry, shaking his head.

Charlie was at Henry's desk, filling his best pen with ink and using his best stationary.

"What you want me to say to him, Henry." Asked Charlie.

Henry, el Rico, and the company men stopped in their tracks, waiting for Henry's answer to that question, they were holding their breaths, after all Henry was concerned with the surgery he was performing.

"Oh, for pete's sakes! Charlie, he's your Dad!" Henry had lifted his hand that was holding the needle in the air not to make any mistakes with the stitching while he contemplated Charlie's question... And Charlie.

"Charlie, just write. You went to the best schools money could buy, you do know how to write!" said Henry, shaking his head and trying not to laugh. Simon's well-being was still under the gun. Henry then gave Charlie a look that el Rico has only seen him give the OX as he jumped on his back.

'Oh, oh,' thought el. Rico, 'better get more whiskey and get water on the stove for two hot, hot baths.' In fact he gave that message to Sassy who was hiding behind her apron, so Henry would not see her laughing face. Sassy shook her head in agreement and quietly went out the door, laughing all the way to the kitchen.

Ms Bessie was rocking in the rocker she kept in the kitchen for a coffee break, when she had time, or not, like today, she was dead tired and her feet hurt.

"What you laughing at, Miss Sassy." Asked a tired Ms Bessie.

"Lordy, Lordy, Ms Bessie, you will never believe what I just heard in the library, coming from Mr. Charlie and Mr. Henry's mouths. Please give me just a minute to put two big pots of water on the stove and go into the liquor cabinet to get another bottle of whiskey, they done run out of one." Laughed Sassy as she quickly followed el Rico's instructions.

She quickly fixed herself and Ms Bessie a cup of coffee, as she said, "I just got a minute to be in here, el Rico might need me." But, this is too funny, I can only tell you, Ms Bessie, it's a secret, I think.

Sassy, quickly left the kitchen, while Ms Bessie was just-a-rocking and laughing at the comedy going on and on between Mr. Henry and Mr. Charlie, as usual. "Them boys, them boys." she said.

Sassy, opened the library door as softly as she could, carrying the bottle of whiskey. All was quiet. Mr. Charlie was licking the envelope with the message to his Dad inside.

Henry was making Simon comfortable on the library table as el Rico and two of the men from the lumber company took off the bloody sheets and el Rico wiped the couch with an alcohol rag and clean sheets were put on it. Two men then lifted Simon up with Henry's supervision and put him on the couch with great care while el Rico and Sassy covered him with a blanket to keep him warm. They took the dirty sheets to the back of the house where they would be soaked and scrubbed and ironed for the next time they are needed.

Simon was still asleep and would sleep all the way home. 'It was too soon to move Simon', thought Henry.

"Come in Morris," said Henry as he met him in the hall. "We have a bad situation today." Said Henry as he shook Morris's hand and led him into the dining room across the hall from the Library.

Henry pulled out a chair for Morris and one for himself. He called el Rico into the room and asked him to ask the men from the library to join them and get Sassy to sit with Simon. "Oh, and please bring the new bottle and glasses all around. You can invite Charlie too."

"Are you alright Henry?" Morris was Henry's cousin.

"Well after I got off the Ox, I was better, but I am worn out, we have the "The Harvest" going on, the Sugar Cane "Harvest" that, as you know, takes at least two or three days to do."

"Excuse my manners, Morris, how are you and the family?" Asked Henry.

"Henry, with all you got going on, I can't complain. We are all well and looking forward to Josh's big day, that little boy is the happiest I have ever known about his religion. Mine do really good, but that is not their normal conversation, unless Josh and Ben are around. They say the Rosary when they stop to rest after playing ball, or Jacks, or you name it." Said Morris, "Very good for all the children." he added.

"I know, he has me studying the Catechism just to keep up with his studies. And like we all do, he loves saying the Rosary on the front porch in the evening before we go to bed. Of course Mom and I have always done that with the girls, but Josh starts it. Amazing." Said a proud Uncle Henry."

The dining room door opened and four men came in with el Rico showing them to the table and chairs.

Morris was caught by surprise to see three men from Mr. Charles' company, who he worked for, come into the room, with Amy coming in from the kitchen hallway.

"What is it Henry?" Morris asked.

"Oh Excuse, me Taint' Amy, I didn't see you come in. How are you with all this work going on and so many extra people to see about with the Harvest?"

"Hello Morris, it is so good to see you, the circumstances are a little strained just now, but it will all work out. Please sit down, all of you. Henry pass that whiskey bottle around, please. I sent el Rico to go get something to eat and to rest in his room for an hour. You boys can work that hard, but I will not let you kill el Rico, he will work to death for you."

"Henry, please introduce me to these good men. I think I know all of them now that I take time to look at their faces. How are you and your families?" Asked Amy as she sat down to sip the sherry Gloria brought her. "Thank you, Mon Cher'. Thank you my dear."

"Mama, have you seen Charlie?" Asked Henry.

"Why yes, he was on his way to take a hot bath in his room, with el Rico following him. I told el, not to come down stairs until he has taken a rest, though he did eat his dinner when he was in the kitchen with Charlie, who ate also. He was starving. He said you overworked everybody, especially him."

"Ha! He's just mad because I wouldn't write a note to his Dad for him," laughed Henry.

"Well friends and family, there was an accident at the logging job on the Red River today while the men were riding the logs down the River. Simon, one of the best loggers, rammed the Jig (Pick) through his foot, in between the big toe and the second toe. Good thing it wasn't further on top of the foot, he would have lost the foot for sure." Explained Henry as he sipped his whiskey.

"Oh no," said several voices.

"Afraid so," said Henry. "Since I have the Harvest going on here, I couldn't leave to take care of any accidents that might happen. So I notified everyone that I would take any patients here at the house."

"So Simon was brought here for surgery. The surgery went well and Simon is in the library having a long nap. He has been through the surgery for about two hours now, and Morris, we sent for you to bring him home. We have no more room here just now, and his home is only a few minutes from here. Any questions?" Asked Henry as Charlie came into the room, fed, bathed, powdered, and ready for company and his share of the Whiskey.

"Friends, you all know Charlie, gee you smell good, Charlie." Laughed a dirty, tired, hungry Henry.

"Don't start with me, Henry." Laughed Charlie. "I worked hard for you today."

"I know, Charlie, we really appreciate it, too." Said Henry as he poured Charlie a drink.

"Grab, your glasses men; let's go check on Simon. I think Morris can take him home to his family where he will be fine. I'm sending two drams of pain medicine with you to give to his wife, to give Simon as he needs it. She just needs to give the first one in four hours and the other one, six hours later. I will take a ride out in the morning to check on him." Said Henry as he opened the door to the Library.

Sassy was on the job and when questioned about how Simon was, she said he hadn't moved all afternoon.

"Good" said Henry.

"Charlie, you got that note to send to your Dad? Morris can take it to him if you're staying here tonight."

"Mr. Henry, we hate to interrupt, but we will be going back to the camp and give the news of how Simon is. We will help Morris put Simon into the back seat of the car." Said Elroy.

"Sure, go right ahead men. Charlie are you staying?" Asked Henry.

"Yes, we are having steak tonight, I've been told." said Charlie, "You know I can't refuse steak at Idle Wile'. Thank you Henry."

"Charlie, I got to go take a bath, el Rico, brought my hot, hot, bath water upstairs and I'm more than ready, if you will excuse me for a while, I'll be back as soon as possible. I want to go look for Lil' Wolf and his Tribe and see how the harvest is going."

"Relax Henry, Lil' Wolf and his Tribe of braves and maidens crushed all the stalks of sugar cane." Said Charlie, he had more news to share with the porch rockers and swingers.

"The Maidens were cleaning up the mess of the cane stalks, and pulp, along with any other mess created as the job moved along for today. They will return tomorrow to crush more of the cane. The crushing of the cane is the hardest job of the Harvest. Not taking into consideration, also, the big job of the boiling of the juice that had been extracted from the cane stalks. This will be accomplished also by the Maidens and Braves, with the help of the Arrington family and friends from town. This harvest will take the best part of a week or two."

"They had taken off for a swim and a good meal, with the baskets of food Ms Bessie and the kitchen help had all packed-up for them, which included a bucket of root beer."

"Ms Bessie had asked Lil' Wolf and he completely loved the idea, so, after their swim in the bayou, Lil' Wolf and his Tribe left Idle Wile' with enough food and cake to share and enjoy with the village.

"So then, Lil' wolf said we will see him tomorrow." Continued Charlie with this news.

Lil' Wolf and his Maidens and Braves will return each day until the Harvest was complete.

"They were tired but happy to have accomplished that hard, hot job for Idle Wile' and the other plantations. He said he was looking forward to the Tribes' share of the sugar; he loves sugar. Lil Wolf also said that Henry would know how much his Father, Wild Eagle, would enjoy the beef and the cake, they would share with the Tribe tonight."

"So Henry you can relax over your bath. I'm going to enjoy my drink on the porch, come get me when you're finished or join me, good friend." Said Charlie.

"That's a good plan," said Henry. "I'm on my way upstairs, see you in a while."

"Hey, Jerome, come join me, this porch is great, this time of day." Said Charlie.

"Thanks Charlie. Man, this Harvest has me beat, today." Said Jerome as he got comfortable in a rocking chair. Jerome had grabbed a bath in the barrel in the barn with lots of soap, clean towels, and clean clothes from the shelf of clean clothes kept in the barn.

"Have a glass of whiskey, Jerome, or we have lemonade." Said Ms Bessie, standing at the screen door until Jerome settled down on the rocker.

"Hello, gentlemen, mind if I join you?" Asked Ms. Amy, as she sat on the swing with her petite glass of Sherry.

"Hello, hello, everyone, I'm joining the porch loafers, if I may." Said a clean Henry.

The steak dinner was delicious and so were the many deserts lined up on the side-board table in the dining room.

The children were bathed and dressed in their gowns and white socks on their feet, all ready for the Rosary on the porch and bed time.

They were all quiet after dinner, rocking and swinging on the porch.

Henry drew out his Rosary from its little leather pouch. The children picked up their Rosary's where they were kept, on the table at the door of the hall.

Jay, Charlie, and Jerome all had their Rosary's in their pocket, for when they were needed.

Charlie led the Rosary in Thanksgiving for not getting mauled by the 'Beast' the Ox.

Each prayed for their own devotion to the Blessed Mother and Her Son, Jesus.

Good Night. Sweet Dreams. WHEW!

Chapter Eleven

"THE PROPOSAL"

Bailey, Ethel M.T.

Henry proposed to Katherine while at a Dinner for Two (and a chaperone at the next table).

Henry had asked his Mother to make the arrangements: white Flowers and a Special Table at Antoine's French Restaurant downtown in New Orleans. It was a very Romantic Evening.

Henry held Katherine's hand and placed a Two Caret Diamond ring on her finger as he kneeled on the carpet and asked her. "Will you please, Marry Me Katherine?"

Katherine looked at Henry and with a wicked smile on her beautiful face said: "I doubt it, Henry; I have known you too long".

Before Henry could faint, his face had turned pale, and his blue eyes were greener than blue, Katherine Said:

"Of Course I will love to Marry you, Henry. I thought you would never ask, sometimes you acted like you didn't even know me or like me." Said a laughing, Joyful Katherine.

Henry pulled himself off the floor, as Katherine was standing beside him and he kissed her for the first time, like he had never dared to before.

"Man, Katherine, you almost killed me. I never expected that from my Proposal. I know you are a Minx, but, Honey, where did you come up with that answer." Asked Henry, who was over-joyed at Kathrine's Final answer and he wasn't letting her out of it.

"Oh, Henry, I have waited for this night for so long, all through College, and all through the Rex Pageant, Parade and Ball. I thought for sure you would think that was a Special Time in our lives, but No., I cried on my pillow, till I looked like a 'Frog', in the morning. Mother and Lois thought I was sick. Poppa knew what it was; he took me riding for an Ice Cream Cone, his answer for all my life long miseries."

"Kiss me again, and again and again, Darling Henry, Laughed a Bewitching Katherine.

"Oh, Katherine, I could not have heard sweeter words, my darling, come here." Said Henry.

The Chaperone had left, when Henry got on his knees. She knew what was on Henry's mind and her eyes were full of Happy Tears, for her two favorite people. She was Tuante' Alice, Henry's God Mother, Amy knew how to pick the Special people in Henry's life exactly when he needed them most, even, when he was a new born baby for his Baptism.

"Thank you Mama," said Henry, under his breath, as he kissed his beloved over and over again just as Katherine had asked him to.

Henry and Amy had coffee very early the next morning to talk about, what else, Katherine, and her answer to Henry's Proposal of Marriage.

Henry had hardly slept last night and he wanted to tell his Mother how he went to Tanti' Alice Marie's apartment in the French Market to tell her, "Thank You," with a bouquet of roses for her help at the Restaurant, last night.

Then Henry went into the Chapel of the Saint Louis Cathedral to 'Thank God,' for such a perfect partner for the rest of his life. The Chapel was so quiet and beautiful with the loads of flowers around the Altar, the hundreds of candles lit by worshipers, praying for Special Intentions or in Thanksgiving for Favors Granted, of The Blessed Virgin Mary, as Henry, himself was there to light candles and to pray for Katherine and their families.

He also Thanked God for Josh and his Holy Sacraments, in December, that would join him to his family as a Catholic, as well.

Henry was telling Amy of last evenings events, when Charlie came into the kitchen looking for a cup of Coffee. He had had one cup in bed, but he needed another one after all the commotion of the day before, he found it hard to wake up or go back to sleep, so he got dressed and came downstairs to the kitchen, where Henry and Amy were having their coffee.

"Good Morning, early risers," Said Charlie. "I need more coffee to wake up with this morning. Man, we really had some go-in' ons, Yesterday; with that Hard Headed OX, I thought that day would never end. I'm so glad to be able to have some quiet time, for all of us. I am so glad the Uncles and the Share Croppers, are harvesting the vegetables, nuts, fruit, and other crops." Said a tired Charlie.

Amy was fixing more cups of coffee, when Ms Bessie came into the kitchen to start the days' work of meals for the family, the workers, and the servants. Just another day on the Farm. 'Well Thank God, the Sugar Cane Harvest was over,' she thought as she met Sassy at the door and they went into the Kitchen together. Well, the Kitchen was already full of family and friends.

Henry and Charlie said "Good Morning" to Bessie and Sassy, and they took their fresh coffee out to the Front Porch to rock and swing and enjoy the morning.

Amy followed the men and claimed her place on the swing, the one with her special pillow for her back, when resting.

"Charlie, how are you, this morning?" Asked Amy. "Did you sleep alright during the night?"

"Yes Ma'am, Ms. Amy, I slept fine, just not enough. You know how hard Henry works everybody especially me and that Ole' Ox." Replied Charlie, knowing exactly what he was going to get from Henry.

Man was he ever surprised at Henry and Amy's laughing faces after his remarks.

"Charlie, my boy," said Henry, "You do not know what is happening during the night when you are sleeping!" Amy just couldn't help herself, she just burst out laughing and spilled her coffee all over that clean porch floor.

"My, My, My, Ms. Amy, must be quite a story. No, I guess I don't know what is happening during the night here at Idle Wile', while I am sleeping. What exactly is happening?" Asked a wide eyed Charlie. He always thought he knew everything about Idle Wile'. Particularly when he was there. Well, obviously not.

Henry filled Charlie in, on last night's events concerning his proposal to Katherine.

Henry and Charlie were looking at each other in amazement at what Henry has accomplished with Amy's help, the night before.

"Engaged? Huh! Well, I am very happy for you. I always thought Katherine was the girl for you, Henry. She is beautiful, smart and happy all the time and Catholic. What a perfect lady for you, I am happy for you, Henry." Said a surprised Charlie or maybe just taken by surprise.

"When is the Wedding? Soon I hope," said Charlie, "I hate waiting for important Events to come along. No Patience, I guess."

"No patience, I know, Charlie." Said Henry. "But, I'm kind of the same way, especially, now that I have Katherine's answer, and it's 'Yes', I really don't want a long engagement and neither does she. We live too far apart for that, I don't see enough of her as it is." Declared Henry.

Amy came through the screen door carrying a tray of coffee cups and biscuits for Henry, Charlie and herself.

"Thank you Ma'am," said Charlie and Henry, while taking a buttered biscuit with their cup of coffee.

"Well, I will go get Katherine after the Hunt and we can make wedding plans. Is this O.K. with you, Mama?" Asked Henry.

"Why, yes said Amy, I will be happy to have her and Louisa', too, if she wants to come", smiled Amy.

"Well, I'm going see about the boys, I'll let Henry tell you about last night, after bed time, Charlie." Teased Amy, as she got up, wiped the coffee from the porch floor with a rag, and went indoors.

"Good, I'll send Katherine a note by Johnny today," decided Henry.

"Hi Johnny, it is so good to see you, Sir." Ms. Jane welcomed the young horse- back rider from the Idle Wile' Farm.

"Good Morning, Ms. Jane. Mr. Henry has sent a message to Ms. Katherine and Ms. Louisa', today". Replied Johnny, removing his cap.

"You know Johnny; I just have to see your wonderful horse coming down the rode to know that 'Henry or Charlie' has sent a message to the girls.' You are a true and faithful friend of both families.

"Yes Mam, Thank you very much." Blushed Johnny. Although this is the welcome he receives from all the members of the families he knows and his work involves. Thank the Good Lord, thought Johnny.

"It's my pleasure. Ms. Jane."

"Well, come on in, Shirley, come see who's here, and I am sure he would appreciate a cup of coffee and a good, breakfast or lunch, maybe." Said Jane, checking with Johnny for his preference and then looking at Shirley.

"Yes, Ms. Jane", said Shirley. "Come on in the kitchen, Johnny and I'll fix a hot meal, what would you like, this morning?" Asked Shirley, smiling at Ms. Jane and Johnny.

"Ms. Jane, may I fix you a cup of coffee?" Asked Shirley, cocking her head toward Jane.

"Yes, thank you. I will have it on the porch, are the girls out there, this morning?"

"Yes, Mam," answered Shirley.

"Thank You, Shirley, I'm sure all three of us on the porch, would like another cup of coffee. Thank you." Said Ms. Jane, as she said good-bye to Johnny, and, he handed her the note for Katherine.

Shirley heard the screen door, shut, and then she asked Johnny,

"O.K. Johnny, what's the news at the Farm, while I'm frying eggs for you, have a seat right here by me."

"Shirley, I don't know anything from the Farm this morning. All I know is, Mr. Jerome came to my room and woke me up, and no coffee, and said Mr. Henry had a chore for me. Then I saddled up and rode to town to bring a message. That's all I know. Thank you for the eggs and biscuit." Smiled Johnny.

"Good morning, Girls," Said Jane, as she kissed each one of her daughters on the forehead.

"Good Morning, Mother", said the girls, returning her kiss on her cheek.

"What did Johnny want, this early in the morning?" Asked Louisa'.

"A message for Katherine, Honey", Answered Jane.

"Humph, I knew IT," Said Louisa' after the news she is holding back from me until you could join us, Mother, Must be Henry, if it's from Idle Wile'"

Just then the Screen Door opened and Shirley placed a tray on the little table in front of the girls on the swing and Jane sitting on the wicker chair, near-by.

"Thank You, Shirley. Is Johnny having his breakfast?"

"Yes, Mam, he was hungry and thirsty, after that early morning ride. But he is resting now."

"Well, good, Shirley. I think Katherine will have a return message for him as soon as she can read the note and decide what she wants to do. AND I decide what she can Do!" Laughed Jane and Louisa'.

Katherine made a face like a kitten, just waking up from a nap. Not too pleased with the comment from her Mother, however true it was.

"Excuse me Please, Mother." Said Katherine, as she removed herself from the swing and went to the rocker that was in the far corner of the porch.

Jane and Louisa', watched Kathrine, over their coffee cups, as Katherine read and re-read her note. Katherine held the note in her hand and looked at the beautiful flowers and trees planted along the Boulevard and yard of her home.

Katherine, moved slowly to the swing, and sat down by Louisa'.

'Well,' thought Katherine I guess it's time to tell the Good News. I better get Dad here before,' though, wisely thinking, Katherine.

"Well, Mom and Louisa', I want to get Dad, here before I share this News with all of you," Said Katherine, to her family on the swing, as she picked up her cup of coffee.

Louisa' left the swing, and ran across the porch and jumped off the edge of the porch and disappeared down the sidewalk on the side of the house, toward the back yard.

"That child is always so dignified", Grinned her Mother. Katherine smiled and shook her head in agreement.

They were all sitting on the porch with their coffee, while Katherine opened her note from Henry to read it to the family.

"Well, Henry writes, that Ms. Amy has invited the family to Idle Wile', after Henry and Charlie Boy are back from the Hunt, to talk about Josh's Baptism and Holy Communion on Christmas Eve., in the St. Louis Cathedral."

"Amy also wants to have a Family Party to Celebrate, Me and Henry's Engagement."

"What do you think Mom and Dad?" Asked Kathrine

The Front porch 'Exploded', with surprise and speechlessness!! Except from Louisa'.

Father stood up and spilled his coffee.

"What, what"? Katherine, are you serious. Honey, you are not the daughter with sudden surprises?" He barked.

'Oh, oh', thought Katherine, Father never barks, even at Louisa's surprises.

"My, My," said Louisa', did you have a chaperone, last night?"

"Of course, Louisa', you know we did, Tante' Alice, had Dinner with Henry and I." Scowled Katherine at her little sister.

"Louisa', behave yourself." Fussed Mama.

"'This is a very Special Day for Katherine. Louisa', go ask Shirley to bring a tray of coffee to us, please." Said Mama.

"Oh, Mama, I am so sorry, I was just surprised and that just came out of my mouth, I am so sorry, Katherine, I didn't mean that." Cried Louisa', who never wanted to upset her family, she loved so much.

"Mama, I'm sorry too, I didn't know how to tell you, of Henry's Proposal, so I just blurted it out. I know there was a better way. Henry's note just took me by surprise." Said Katherine.

Shirley opened the door carrying the much needed cups of coffee, more than she knew.

Everyone was hugging and kissing Katherine, Louisa' was holding onto Katherine's hand.

"Thank you Shirley, we have just had some good news from Idle Wile'." Said Mama.

"Katherine, I think that is a fine idea, you and Louisa' can go to Idle Wile' after the Hunt, and Dad and I can follow. We have a few things to take care of here before we can go for a visit to Idle Wile'."

"O.K., Mom, sounds good to me." Said Katherine.

"How about you, Louisa'?" Asked Katherine.

"Sounds good to me," said Louisa', "can we take the horses?"

"Louisa' we can send the horses to the Farm, I wouldn't like the idea of you, and Katherine riding them all the way to the Farm, if that's what you're asking." Answered her Father.

"That's O.K. Dad, I don't want my horse there, and Henry has more than enough horses to ride at the Farm." Said Katherine, for Louisa', too." She added.

"O.k., O. K.," Laughed Louisa', your right Kathrine, I was just thinking of all the trails and the big forest to ride in, that would be fun with Tiger along."

"Well, I think we will have enough to do, while we are there, without having to bother with feeding and taking care of the horses, too." Said Katherine.

"Katherine, it's you, Henry and Josh's time to be the center of attention, not Tiger's." Laughed Louisa'. "I'll be fine just to be with you and the family."

"O.K.," said Katherine we are all set. Let me write a note to Henry for Johnny to take back to the Farm, and let him know we are coming after he and Charlie are back from the Hunt."

Johnny took the note from Ms. Jane and was on his way back to the Farm, with the good news.

Chapter Twelve

"CEREMONIAL PLANS"

Bailey, Ethel M.T.

"Josh, don't wake up your Uncle, He was out late last night, taking care of your big day!" Said el Rico, as he came into Henry's room with a cup of coffee and a biscuit.

"Shush, I know, Mr. el. I am so excited, I just want to lay down by him so I can be here when he wakes up, I promise. Said Josh.

"O.K. Josh, no noise, I'll help you get into the bed, but you stay on the other side, you hear Me.?" Asked el Rico. "I'm going get your cup of coffee and a biscuit, be quiet. No talking."

"Yes, Sir, Thank You." Said a quiet Josh.

el Rico had just left the room when a soft tap sounded on the closed door.

"Who is it?" whispered Josh as he leaned against the door.

"Josh, is that you? I've been looking all over this floor for you, what are you doing in Mr. Henry's room, at this time in the morning honey, Asked Gloria, Josh's Nanny.

"Oh Nanny, I am so excited, I just had to come see Uncle Henry, even if he is asleep." Explained Josh.

"I'm coming out, Nanny, we will wake up Uncle if we keep on talking", said Josh, as he slowly opened the door and stepped out into the hall, of the Mansion on St. Charles Ave.

And Henry Woke Up!

Nanny was helping Josh dress for the day. It was time for Breakfast with Amy, Ben, and the Girls.

The family was still in New Orleans. Henry, Katherine, Jane, and Amy, had an appointment with Father Theriot. This was a planning appointment to make arrangements for the two ceremonies, Baptism and First Communion for Josh and for Henry and Katherine's wedding ceremony.

There was the job of the Decorations for the Cathedral for Mid Night Mass. There are protocols for how the Catholic Church has to be decorated for The Holy Mass for all Seasons, for all Masses. All of these arrangements had been completed last night.

The Mass is in Father's Hands, as always and the Flowers and decorations are in Mrs. Bennett's competent hands, with Father Theriots' approval, of course.

Katherine and Henry were sitting on the front porch of the St. Charles Ave. Home of Katherine's family.

The couple was at home, where other family members were around, so there was no need for a Chaperone.

Henry had a problem accepting these rules, since he and Katherine were engaged and were planning the Wedding in a couple of weeks. He just wanted to get close to Katherine; he needed to feel her hair and to hold her, as they made plans to go to England on the Queen Mary for their Honeymoon. Henry needed lots of attention, now that he knew Ms K, really loved him. He stayed excited. And Charlie was soooo jealous, it tickled Henry. He loved Charlie, but as a friend, not at all like he loved Katherine.

"Well, hello people. How is my favorite couple, asked Charlie? As he walked up the steps to the porch.

"Got room for one more on that swing?" Charlie was bond and determined to make Henry mad, in front of Katherine.

But, Henry was smarter than that. He looked at Katherine and let her answer Charlie's question, it was not the answer he was expecting from Katherine.

"Sure, Charlie, any friend of Henry's, is a friend of mine. Come we have room right here, by Me." she said, as the thunder clouds blew over Henry's face.

"Oh no, Katherine, I really came looking for Louisa', I was hoping she could go boating with me on the Lake, this afternoon. It is just a beautiful, today." Said Charlie.

"Charlie Boy, don't forget the Chaperone", laughed Henry. He couldn't help it. He just loved Charlie-Boy. 'Man I got to learn to read Charlie's sense of humor. He knew he'd 'got Me."

"Henry, you and Katherine want to come out on the Lake, if Louisa' can come?" Asked Charlie

"I'd like to Charlie, but I am packing this afternoon, to leave town, for a few days. Louisa' is coming with me." Said Katherine as she watched, Henry's expression, not Charlie's.

"This must be an emergency," said Henry. "Where are you going? How long you going to be gone, we're getting married in a couple of weeks, Katherine, remember? Can I come, too?" Asked a puzzled Henry.

"I'm sorry Henry, I was going to tell you as soon as we got settled on the swing, but then Charlie walked up the sidewalk. I didn't have a chance, yet." Apologized Katherine.

"Opps, Sorry Katherine and Henry, I thought you were just having coffee or dessert. " Apologized Charlie, nicely.

"That's O.K. Charlie, we always glad to see you, we just been busy with the Harvest, Josh's Baptism and Holy Communion and then the Wedding. Which we are all glad of, these occasions' happening now. We wouldn't change it for the world, huh Katherine? There seems to be fewer and fewer hours in the day, somehow, just now." Explained Henry.

"By the way, I did ask you to be my 'Best Man." What is your answer?" Teased Henry.

"Henry, I said 'NO' remember?" Said Charlie, with his head down, looking at the floor of the porch.

"You did Not, Charlie!" Yelled Henry. "You said 'Sure you would like to."

"Your right, Henry, I'm sorry, I don't know what came over me." Said Charlie.

Just then, Louisa' came out onto the Porch and sat on the rocker.

"Hi Charlie, I thought I heard your voice. You catching up on all the news, and happening around here?" She asked.

"Henry and Katherine sure took 'No Time', in making up their minds."

"Only years, Louisa', what you talking about?" Teased Henry.

"Well, looks like Josh's excitement about his Baptism and First Communion, sparked a lot of other announcements. I am so happy for all of you. Josh is over the moon about his coming events with the Catholic Church. I am very happy for him. Henry, I got him a new saddle for his Indian Pony that Lil' Wolf is giving him as a present. He named the pony, Lil' Jo." Said Charlie.

"He will love that, present. Thank You, Charlie." Said Henry.

"Louisa' and I are giving him a new coat for this winter. It is really cold when you travel in a buggy in the Winter time in New Orleans." Said Katherine, looking at her sister, Louisa', who was in agreement.

"What are you giving him, Henry?" Asked Louisa'.

"Well, Mama is giving him a new Prayer Book of the Daily Mass and I'm giving him a new pair of Leather Boots." Said Henry. "I heard Mama say that all the Uncles and Aunts and the Servants and Sheriff Jay, and God Knows who else are giving him, presents, too.

"His Nanny is giving him a sweater. Ms Bessie and Sassy are giving him books. I don't know what the rest of the people are giving him. He will be so surprised and happy." Laughed Henry.

"Mama, Louisa' and I are going into New York on the train, tomorrow, we will be gone three nights. I want a special wedding dress and I can't get it around here." Blushed Katherine.

"Well, Katherine Charlie and I can pick you, Louisa' and your Mother up, to meet the Train at the Station, if you want us too?" Said Henry.

"Oh, I am so sorry, Henry, said Katherine. But Father has decided he will bring us to the Train Station. We will have our three Maids with us, and you know how many carriages we will need for all of us to go to New York.

"Yes. We are really looking forward to the trip of 'High Shopping', with Father paying the Bills." Laughed Louisa'.

"As usual, little girl," smiled Katherine", don't let Mama hear you say that, honey, she will cut your allowance. Of course, Papa will give it back to you with a bonus. He's so sweet on you and me and Mama, too. All His Girls, he says."

"Yep, just as it should be, laughed Louisa'.

"Well, Henry and Charlie, we hate to cut this visit short, but, we better go pack our cases. Papa is having the stable boys pick them up early in the morning. Casey is taking one buggy of luggage to the train, early, before we go at the scheduled boarding time. I got a hunch; Papa will come with us at the last minute. Mama is packing his luggage just in case." Laughed Katherine.

"Well, bye Honey," said Henry as he gave her a peck on the cheek, while holding her hand.

"Be careful, there Romeo," Laughed Charlie", you might get caught, as he gave Louisa' a peck on the cheek, too.

"Charlie, you the one that better be careful, I'm engaged to Katherine, remembers?" Said Henry.

"Yes, you are right; Henry, Louisa', and I have an understanding." Laughed Charlie.

"Yes, Not to be so bold and try to take advantage of me, I got Katherine with me." Said Louisa'.

"We'll see you when we get back," said Katherine.

"Yes, said Henry as he and Charlie walked down the side-walk home.

"Let's get a sandwich and a cup of coffee, Charlie, I'm hungry!

"Sounds great Henry, I missed Lunch." Said Charlie.

"Let's get the Kids and Mama and say the Rosary this afternoon, Charlie. I'm still tired and I want to take a long nap that might last until tomorrow morning. Smiled Henry.

As the Sandwich's and Lemonade were brought to the porch, the children came out to Swing and watch the Streetcars go by.

The Sandwich's were delicious and were gone in a few bites, by Charlie and Henry and the children, who are always hungry.

"Nap," Ben asked", but we just woke up from our afternoon nap."

"Oh, well, Charlie and I haven't so we are going to take a nap, a long quiet one."

"Bella, would you like to lead the Rosary?" Asked Amy, as she handed the children their Prayer Beads.

"Yes, Mam." Answered Bella, as she straightened out her Rosary and found the Cross.

"In the Name of The Father." Bella's sweet, gentle, young little voice started, almost in a whisper. The rest of the porch sitters concentrated on their Rosary, One Prayer bead at a time.

Good Evening Dear Friends.

Chapter Thirteen

"OLE' MAN RIVER"
(the Skull)

Bailey, Ethel M.T.

When the Mississippi River below New Orleans, down the Delta Route of Louisiana, reaches low-tide many secrets are exposed.

Take the time for instance, when a thirteen year old boy named John Ed, a little friend of Henrys', and whose Dad was Foreman on the Plantations Henry Family owned, went fishin' with his little brother, Sidney.

John Ed and his younger brother, Sidney, were out looking for a fishing spot along the banks of that Ole' Muddy River. They had their old cane poles all strung up and baited with tantalizing Louisiana shrimp. (Ask us, we'll tell you, fish can't refuse it, Yummm.)

Anyway, they wanted to catch a fresh-water catfish big enough for dinner at home.

"Oh, my goodness!" yelled John Ed to Sidney.

"Oh no, no, no," stammered Sidney.

"That, that, looks like a head, I ain't staying with no head sticking out the water." Yelled Sidney.

"Let's get out of here, John Ed!" Yelled Sidney as he ran past his brother, almost knocking him down into the Ole' Muddy in the process.

Now the "skull" was looking straight at the boys, uh, uh, uh, not good.

"WOAH," shouted John Ed, sweating as much as Sidney. His eyes were as big as saucers and were beginning to have very large tears running down his cheeks.

"We gotta go tell the Sheriff, Sidney." Yelled John Ed.

"OHhhhhh, NO," cried Sidney, "We ain't gonna tell no Sheriff, we gonna go get Henry, that's who, and he can tell the Sheriff," laughed Sidney, wiping his tears on his sleeve.

'Poor Henry,' thought John Ed, 'he gets it all. Well, he is The Boss. Huh, so, just as well.'

Running faster than fast, they took a hard left toward the Plantation, standing in the morning sunshine.

Nobody knew what was about to hit all the inside and outside and around the countryside.

"John Ed, Sidney! Where you boys going?" Asked Henry, while putting his arms around the crying and scared boys. Henry knew these boys; they were boys whose family worked for the Plantations, their Father was Foreman of the Corn Fields.

"Mr. Henry, we came looking for you after what we saw in the river bed. We were looking for a place to fish on the river side of Idle Wile'."

"The river is at low tide where we were looking for a good place to fish and then we, 'Saw IT! A terrible sight, just terrible, on the river's bottom at low tide. We saw, we Saw", Sidney could not stop crying, so Henry asked John Ed to tell them what they saw, so that Henry would know what to do."

"Mr. Henry, we saw a "SKULL" on the bottom of the river where the tide had gone out. We didn't know what to do; we were so scared of that old skull's eyes looking straight at us."

"I wanted to go tell the Sheriff, Mr. Jay, but Sidney, he said no-way. We gonna' go tell you, Mr. Henry."

"I'm not messing with no Sheriff. My Pa would skin us for sure." Yelled Sidney.

"O. K., O.K, boys, slow down." Said Henry.

"Josh, you and Noah, please help me pick up the fishing tackle and take it to the barn, be careful of the hooks, they are very dangerous." Said Henry

"John Ed, you and Sidney go tell Mr. I.J. what has happened so he can get hold of your Dad from out in the fields. Don't tell anyone else what you saw, it will be bad enough when I tell Sheriff Jay why I'm looking for him." Said Henry.

"Now, go boys, after you tell Mr. I.J. and, stay at Idle Wile'. We will see you there, in a little while. John Ed, you and Sidney stay with Josh and Ben, and only tell Ms. Amy, after Mr. I.J., what you just told me. O.K. Boys?" Asked Henry.

Henry went to the stables to find Jerome, concerning the skull in the river bottom.

"Jerome, I need to talk to you for a minute. Meet me on the front porch in a few minutes, if you have time." Said Henry.

"Sure, Mr. Henry, I'll be there in a few minutes. Would you like a cup of coffee?"

"I sure would Jerome that would hit the spot." Smiled Henry, as he walked across the yard to the front porch.

Jerome came a few minutes later with two cups of hot-fresh coffee. He handed one to Henry and he sat on a rocker to talk.

"You and the boys not fishing today?" Asked Jerome.

"I'm afraid we ran into a problem concerning the river at low tide. John Ed and Sidney were going fishing on the river side of the Plantation and discovered to their horror a "SKULL" stuck in the mud and, as they say, 'was looking straight at them'. Two scared little boys ran straight to us with this problem." Said Henry, while sipping his coffee.

"Mr. Henry, I know what that 'Skull" in the river bed is all about." Said Jerome.

"Well, Jerome, I hope it is not the horror story we think it is. I don't remember any tales of 'a skull' in the Mississippi River or any sighting of "skulls" in any body of water around here."

"What's the story?" Jerome.

"Well, years ago, when Jean Lafitte was first in these parts, he had many fights with the Indian Tribes who thought they owned the river and the land all around it. The old timers tell the story of fights between the Indian Tribes and Jean Lafitte and his Pirates." Said Jerome as he sipped his coffee.

"Come on the porch, Mama, we have a very interesting story going on here." Said Henry, as Amy came out to the porch with her glass of lemonade.

"Thank you Henry, I didn't know you two were out here." Said Amy.

"Well, Mama, did the boys tell you of John Ed and Sidney finding the skull on the river bottom, this morning?" Asked Henry.

"Yes, they did. John Ed and Sidney were pretty scared; seeing that Skull like that." Said Amy.

"Ms Bessie took the boys home to their Mama and a hot bath and dinner to settle them down. I hope you agree with that decision. I decided they had had enough excitement for one day." Said Amy.

"I did the same thing with Josh and Ben; they were wide eyed and troubled."

"Jerome, go ahead with your story of the "skull" in the river bed." Said Henry.

"Well, like I said, the Indian Tribes did not take kindly to Jean Lafitte coming into the river with his big boats and taking over the land along the shore."

"Jean Lafitte had a different idea of 'finder's keepers, loser's weepers,' this is what the old timers tell all the town families that's what happened. Well, the Chitimacha and the Biloxi Tribes did not agree with the Pirate. So when Lafitte landed his boats on the river the next time, the Tribes were ready for him."

"The Tribes built huge, high bon- fires along the shore so they could see the boats of Lafitte coming into the river at night, as he did most of the time, when he came to the shores of Louisiana from the Mississippi River."

Fire on the River

"The Indians lit those fires just as Lafitte had his boats docked and tied to stakes in the mud and the anchors imbedded in the bottom of the river and his men on shore."

"Then, the Indians struck the Pirates and Jean Lafitte as they were building cooking fires of their own and bathing in the river. The Pirates did not know what or who hit them. But Jean Lafitte, who always keeps at least twenty-five men on board the ships just in case of trouble on shore, jumped the ropes in the mud and cut them with his saber, yelled to his men on shore to board the boats and he managed to save two of his boats and treasure and most of his 'Jolly Pirates'."

"However, the Indians had the last word. They captured two of the boats loaded with treasure, food, and liquor. They killed about twenty or more pirates that Lafitte left on the river bank and most of them landed in the river as an Indian arrow struck them as they tried to fight the Warriors."

"Ever since then, every few years, a 'skull' shows up on the bottom of the river, at low tide. It's just a shame that John Ed and Sidney had to spot it while looking for a good fishing spot."

"We haven't seen or heard of any for a number of years, until today. I am so sorry the boys had to find that one. I hope this story and adventure will entertain the boys and help them to forget their adventure of the "skull" incident." Said Jerome as he finished the history of the 'skull' found in the river and his cup of coffee.

"Thank you Jerome, it sure is good to have that mystery solved for the boys, and any new comers to this area, who have not heard of this story before, like the Arrington family." Said Henry.

"Yes," said Amy, "this story will go around the country side and the towns for weeks".

"Jerome, you will be here for dinner I hope. We have roasted deer meat tonight." Said Amy.

"Yes Mam, thank you, Ms Amy." Answered Jerome, who is always ready for the taste of deer meat cooked by Ms Bessie.

After dinner, the boys wanted to hear the story of the "skull" found in the river bed that morning.

Jerome told the story again, making it a little gentler because of the age of the boys and girls listening to it, around the front porch rockers and swings.

"Time for the Rosary," said Amy, as Henry and Jerome reached into their pockets for their Rosary Beads. The children had theirs on the little table by the door where Amy put them each evening.

"May God Bless the Souls of the Indians and the Pirates of the river bed grave." Said Henry, at the end of the Rosary. "In The Name of The Father, and Of The Son, and Of The Holy Spirit, Amen." Said the family.

Good Night, Good Friends.

Chapter Fourteen

"PLANS FOR MIDNIGHT MASS"

Bailey, Ethel M.T.

It was so cold in the French Quarter that Monday evening. The beautiful tall, old gas-street lanterns were lit by the Lamp Lighter every evening.

The Square was filled with twilight; there has been no sunshine today.

You could look down the narrow streets of Jackson Square and see the many black-iron benches following the walk-way of the park. The benches were filled with the many workers of New Orleans, taking a rest in the park.

The big fountain in the center of the sidewalk was surrounded by many beds of roses of many colors. The fountain and its bubbling sound of water could be heard all over the Square. The sound of a small band playing the many songs of New Orleans could be heard as well.

The Cathedral was lit with many bracketed gas lamps along the outside wall. There were big iron candle stick holders, with burning candles, lighting the way up the steps to the giant doors of the church. It was time for the Evening Mass and Prayers.

Katherine, Henry, and their Mothers, Amy and Jane, all attended Mass that Monday evening.

After Mass, the two families have an appointment with Father Theriot and the Professional Decorator of the Cathedral, Ms. Bennett. She has the job of decorating the Cathedral in a Traditional Style, for all Masses and Special Occasions; the floral arrangements were changed each week.

Ms. Bennett is in the meeting to add her ideas and expertise to the discussion and to be sure she understood the decoration requirements of Father Theriot, Henry and Katherine, and their families, for the Cathedral Services.

There is always, on Holy Days and Daily Mass, Traditional Garments the Priest wears and the Colors and Ropes and Scarfs, of the Vestments for each Sunday Mass as well. These traditional Vestments, all have a prayer that is said by the Priest before he puts each one on. This Holy Ritual for God is carried out by each Priest at every Mass of the Week, Holy Days, and Sundays, in every Catholic Church throughout the World. There is no difference, no matter what day or where the Mass is celebrated.

Mass was over and Father had changed into his regular Black Suit and White Collar for the meeting with the Arrington Family.

Father Theriot invited the family, and Ms. Bennett, to join him at a nearby Italian Restaurant to talk about the Double Sacraments to take place at Christmas Eve Mass.

"Henry and Ladies. I have all the measurements of the Cathedral we will need to design the floral arrangement, ribbons, and other bouquets for the Blessed Virgin that we will need to discuss the decorations for Mid-Night Mass." Said Father.

"I will leave instructions on the little table in foyer of the Cathedral, as to where we are in case your Fathers wish to join us." Said Father.

"I have missed a couple of meals today and my coffee, so we can do both, enjoy a good a meal and discuss the arrangements. Is that alright with everyone?" Asked Father.

"Yes, Father, we are all ready for dinner. Thank you." Answered Henry.

"I am bringing a little satchel with me that will help us to decide on the special mass arrangements. These drawings are the only ones I have of the interior of the Cathedral. It was provided to me by the architect of the firm who repainted the church last year." Explained father.

"I will be happy to return the drawings and I will take very good care of them." Promised Ms. Bennett as everyone was leaving the church to walk across the Square to Antoine's Restaurant, just across the side street from the Cathedral. This famous New Orleans Restaurant is one of Henry and Charlie's favorite restaurants in the French Quarters of New Orleans. They knew them all.

Father, and members of the two well-known Louisiana families, walked into the restaurant; the Master Chef, came out to greet them.

"Well, Father, what do we owe this honor on this fine winter's Eve?" Asked Chef Champagne, as he shook hands with the men in the group and said hello to the ladies.

"A Baptism and a Wedding." Replied Father as he began to introduce the families to the Chef.

"Wait Father, I know these fine people and customers of Antoine's from the banks of the bayou and the Old River we are half-circled by." Smiled the Chef.

"Please take a table and I will send a waiter to take care of your drinks and dinner.

"I have a special menu today to celebrate the New Season. I hope you will find something you will enjoy on it this special evening." Said Chef Champagne.

"I'm sure we will." Answered Henry, as he pulled out Katherine's and Amy's chair for them. The Chef and Father did the same for the other two ladies.

"Bon' Apetite." said the Chef as he walked back to the kitchen to cook for the many guests in the restaurant.

"Well, it all looks good." said Katherine to her Mother and Amy.

"But I am partial to Oysters Rockefeller and this is the winter time, I'm sure they have them. Oh Yes, here they are, and a salad is good for me." Said Katherine.

"Me too," said Amy, Jane, and Ms Bennett.

"I think I will have the Eggplant Parmesan, one of my favorites here. With a salad, and a glass of red wine, merlot, I think." Said Father.

"That sounds good to me, too." Said Henry. "However, I want the Oysters on the half shell, the half dozen, and the Eggplant Parmesan, and White Wine. Unless the Chef has something else in mind, here he comes." Said Henry watching the Chef as he came to the table with a little menu.

"Well, I have a suggestion for you if you care to try a little meat sauce made with white wine and tomatoes and served with French bread for dipping." Said the Chef.

"Yes," said Henry, "we can all share that new dish. Are you game, my friends?" he asked.

"Yes, indeed!" Was the answer all around.

"Great!" said the Chef, "I will make petit dishes all around for tasting." He smiled as he walked back to the kitchen.

Katherine, Amy, Jane, and Ms. Bennett, had been busy looking at the drawings of the Main Area of the Cathedral, where the Ceremonies would take place, and the Bouquets of Flowers would be the main source of Decorations.

The Center Altar with the Large white Candle and Gold Candlestick Holders would each be draped in a Floral Arrangement. The Alcove of The Blessed Virgin Mary would have a Large, Floral Bouquet. The Entrance of each pew would have a Bouquet and would include Netting and A Large Satin Bow. The Chandeliers would be draped in Flowers, Netting, and Bows.

The Bride and Brides' Maids Bouquets were decided by Katherine and her Mother Jane.

Henry and Amy were concentrating on the Outside Benches and Railings, and the Main Entrance to the Cathedral. With Special Attention being given to the small Chapel, located on the side aisle of the Foyer.

The Families asked for all White and Soft Pink Blush flowers with Lacy Greenery, for the Bouquets of the Christmas Eve Mass. The Floral Bouquets would be of Roses, Gladiola, Lilies, with White Orchids for The Blessed Virgin Mary's Alcove. This will include the Church and the Foyer.

"Ladies, I believe this will take care of the Wedding's Floral Arrangements." Smiled Ms. Bennett.

"Yes." Answered all three ladies. "That sounds great.

"You know, Ms. Bennett, let's just leave the Baby Jesus Cradle where it is, and The Babe will go In the Cradle for Christmas, as Tradition has always had it. Is that alright, Father?" Asked Katherine.

"Yes." Said Father, "I agree, where the Church is concerned, especially with the Traditional Seasons, I must have first approval." Smiled Father.

"Father, also, with all due Respect, we acknowledge the fact that this is Your Domain and we will first get your approval on all decisions to be made before being carried out by these two families concerning the Christmas Eve Mass, as is Church Tradition, and Catholic Church's Custom.

"Yes, that is how it must be, agreed Ms. Bennett. Here are the drawings; I have been doing while we are waiting for our food. The little flowers placed in a little square box are for the Men's lapels, one or two for the Blessed Virgin, is in the white box. One is for the Bridesmaid's; it's in the pink boxes. One for your Mothers, those are in the blue box. All, my dear, are just ideas I got as we were talking. Please take them with you and change or add to any one of them you want me to do. I won't do them as finished bouquets until I get your ideas and the final approval from you." Explained Ms. Bennett

"Father, if you don't mind, I would like to return your little satchel. I have my own drawings of the Cathedral now, from yours, and I am sure I will visit the church when I attend Mass on week-days and Sunday, for more enclose formation, as needed." Said Ms. Bennett

The art work by Ms. Bennett had been going around the table and everyone was amazed at the talent Ms. Bennett has as a florist, but the art work was beautiful and superb. They all said that they could really tell just how beautiful the Cathedral would be for Christmas.

Just as Father was finished drinking his wine, the waiter brought the bill to Henry, he made that request when he first ordered his meal.

Henry paid the bill and gave a tip for the waiter and for the Chef, who was so nice to him and his family.

Henry and the waiter helped the ladies with their warm coats and the group said goodbye, to the Head Waiter, who had called Henry's horse and buggy from the Church's barns.

Henry walked with Father back to the Cathedral's Residence and said, "Goodbye Father, we will see you next Sunday, if not before. Thank you for your generous time and help. Josh is so excited about the Baptism and First Communion and Wedding. So am I. Thank God, for the gifts he has given to my family and friends. God Bless you, Father, and thank you, again, for all your help and understanding."

Father thanked Henry for his family's support of the Cathedral and the general collections. Now with the Wedding, Baptism, and Holy Communion, the Church will be full of your family and friends and other people who do not go to Church except on Christmas and Easter. They will come to enjoy the beautiful flowers flowing throughout the Cathedral and the Baptism and Wedding taking place at the same Mass.

"Henry, I've arranged for a special pew for Lil' Wolf and his family and friends. It's right behind your family and friends. He will have the third pew. I know how you two are close. Is this arrangement O.K. with you and your family?" Asked Father."

"Father, it is more than O.K. It is perfect. Lil' Wolf and his Maiden are coming dressed in white Buck Skin. He is so looking forward to it. He will be staying at the Chitimacha Tribe's Hunting Lodge."

"Thank you Father, for thinking of Lil' Wolf. I am ashamed to say that I forgot to make preparations in the Cathedral for him and his Maiden for the Baptism and Wedding Services."

"The wedding, on the same day as Josh's big day, came as a total surprise to me. I just was not ready for that. It is Katherine's idea and I am so happy about it. Josh is just walking on air. We are all happy about these events taking place in the Cathedral and at Mid-Night Mass."

"Thank you Father. I'd better go get the Ladies. Good Night." Said Henry.

"Good Night Henry, God Bless You and Your Family." Said Father Theriot.

"Katherine, Mama, Ms. Jane, and Ms. Bennett, I am so sorry if I kept you waiting. Father and I had an arrangement to make for a very special guest of ours for Mid-Night Mass." Said Henry.

"Lil' Wolf?" Asked Katherine and Amy at the same time.

"Yes, you are so right, I almost left him out." Said Henry. "But Father took care of it with the seating arrangement to be close to our family in the third pew, with el Rico, Ms Bessie, and Jerome and others. Mamas, please don't let me forget anyone. Oh, Jay, the Sheriff, he is so well and happy to be back at work. Make a list, please Mama"

"Henry, I promise, it will be all taken care of, "said Amy and Katherine agreed.

The buggy was moving right along. Henry had hired a driver, who will take care of the horse and buggy when they reach the house of Katherine and Jane, then Ms. Bennett's house is down the same lane, and then Mama and Henry will be taken to their home on St. Charles. The driver will return the buggy and horse to the stables where he works and after taking care of the horse and buggy he will call it a day and go home too.

"What a long and happy day." Said Amy to Henry.

"I am saying my Rosary in my bed with my gown on and a warm glass of milk," said Amy.

"Me too. Good Night Mama, I hope you sleep well, God Bless You." Said Henry.

Good Night Dear Friends.

Chapter Fifteen

"GIRLS BACK IN NEW ORLEANS"

Bailey, Ethel M.T.

The New York Express Train whistled its way to the train station of New Orleans, on Canal Street.

The train came to a stop near the walkway of the train station on Friday afternoon. Katherine and Louisa' were so excited; they had left Jerome and four of the tain Porters to take the luggage and shopping Boxes from their compartments, and went to the platform car of the train.

The girls had not even consulted, their mother, Jane, as to where they were going. They were headed to the rear of the train, looking for Henry and Charlie in the crowd. Nope, not even a glance of either one of them. 'Uh, Uh, Uh,' thought Katherine.

Someone tipped her wide brim white hat, to look at her face, "Henry", yelled Katherine.

Louisa' had spotted Charlie Boy and turned her back to him, so he could not tip her hat from her face.

Katherine, let Henry give her a peck on the cheek, as Louisa' had a Kiss from Charlie Boy. You cannot fool that boy with a wide brim hat. Or deny him a kiss, taken by surprise.

Jane walked up to the girls, but did not recognize the boys, because she was not looking for them on Board of the train.

They knew the Conductor, of course.

Jerome and the Porters were going down the ramp, loaded with luggage and boxes, on their way to the Luggage wagon that was parked next to the Arrington Carriage.

Luggage Wagon

Henry kissed Jane on the hand and took her Night Case from her to carry to the Carriage. Charlie said Hello to Jane and joined Henry going down the ramp, walking behind Jane and her girls.

Henry asked Jerome to take the Luggage to Ms. Jane's home on St. Charles Ave. and the he could meet them at The Court of Two Sisters on Bourbon St., near the Cathedral. Jerome's sisters owned this beautiful court yard Restaurant.

Amy and Mrs. Bennett, the decorator, was waiting for Jane and the girls at the Restaurant.

The travelers and Henry and Charlie came into the Court Yard and found Amy and Mrs. Bennett, sitting under a cool tree sipping a glass of Tea and waiting for them to get there.

"Good morning, Mama and Mrs. Bennett greeted Henry, while he and Charlie pulled out the chairs from the table for the Ladies to sit down and say hello to their friends.

The waiter brought the Menu's and waited for the drink order from the guest.

After the Dinner orders were given to the waiter, Katherine, asked Mrs. Bennett about the progress of the decorations in the Cathedral for Mid-Night Mass.

"Everything is ordered, the Altar Cloths and the White Runners for the Aisles, have arrived. The Flower Vases are at the Cathedral.

The Flowers will be here on Thursday and will be put on Ice until the Decorators who work with me, are ready to make the Bouquets and place them in place in the church.

"The Invitations were posted and most of our friends have received them." Said Amy.

"Sounds, great", Said Henry, "Charlie and I have shopped already, and have our Tuxedos.

"I shopped for the children's clothes and that is completed, down to the shoes. Said Amy.

"Here's our dinner, let's eat." Said Henry.

After Dinner the Ladies and Girls bid 'Fare-well to the men, and headed home to unpack their New York Bags and to rest.

"Good Night" said Amy, Henry, and Charlie.

A Good Night Sleep was in store for them all, after a restful Rosary with Jesus.

Good Night, Dear Friends.

Chapter Sixteen

"THE HUNT"

Bailey, Ethel M.T.

Henry and Charlie were going back to the Plantations to help the Uncles with the rest of the harvest and to go on another hunt. It's Duck Season.

When Henry and Charlie stopped at Buddy's place, for a good meal and a beer, there were a lot of people in town. They left the horses at the stable to be fed, watered, and rested.

The Sheriff's Jay and Ernest met them at the door with handshakes and slaps-on-the-back, to congratulate Henry for the Wedding that was happening in a few days.

"What are you guys doing here?" Asked Henry.

"We came to check up on each other and try to stir up a duck-hunting party while Jay is here for a few days." Said Ernest.

"You all came at the perfect time, if you have time for a hunting Party." Said Jay, following Ernest's lead.

"Guess what, friends. Charlie and I are going to Idle Wile' to help the Uncles with the harvest of the corn, beans and other vegetable crops, to finish the season's work before the wedding." Said Henry.

"Come back in with us, I'll treat you to a beer or ice tea." Offered Charlie.

"Thanks Charlie, we could do with another drink." Said Jay.

"Hey Buddy, how are you?" Asked Henry, as he and Charlie shook hands with him.

Henry and Charlie went to the window seat and waited till Jay and Ernest came in to sit down before ordering drinks.

Buddy brought two meal cards to the table and the waiters put a fresh table cloth on the table and then set it up with silverware and napkins for the diners.

After Henry and Charlie finished eating and telling everyone goodbye, they went to the stables to collect their horses. Pretty soon they would be on their way to Idle Wile' and the families that were waiting for them.

Henry and Charlie reached Idle Wile' and were just in time to see the Uncles before they went home for the day. The Harvest was just about finished. The corn crib was full.

Hundreds of bushels of string beans had been sold and sent to the canning factory to be processed.

The barns were full of vegetables that would be needed for the winter months, such as potatoes and pecans and other crops that kept well through the fall months. Sweet potatoes were a favorite crop to be stored in the storage houses.

The Harvest was over, except for the cleanup of the fields. Those will be prepared for the spring planting. But for now, everyone was ready for the duck hunt and a long rest for the farm hands.

Jimmie, Bud, and I.J. met Henry and Charlie in the barn yard early the next day. Jay and Ernest were coming down the lawn, walking their horses, as not to disturb the lawn with the hooves of the horses in passing on to the barn yard.

The hunting dogs were ready; they could feel the crisp air and the boots of the hunters getting ready for the Hunting Season.

Henry led the hunters to the back woods of Idle Wile'. All the families were told to stay inside the house for a few hours of the hunt. Accidents happened every year by a stray bullet or two.

Duck on the Water

Not surprising, the hunting party heard a few horses ahead of them. Pretty soon, Lil Wolf and his band of Braves came into sight of the plantation hunting party. They had several ducks tied to their belts, they were really early hunters.

"Good Morning, Lil Wolf." Greeted Henry, Charlie, and the Uncles. "Looks like you have had a lot of luck with your bows and arrows."

"The only way to hunt, my friend Henry." Laughed Lil' Wolf and his Braves. "Your boom, boom sticks, make too much noise, they scare the ducks away, out of your sight." He said.

"You're right, Lil' Wolf, we just got to be faster than the ducks on the wing, to shoot them. We don't kill as many as you and you're Braves, but then, we don't have as many people to feed." Laughed Charlie.

"So far" laughed Bud. "I hear you and your Maiden are coming to Henry's Wedding."

"Yes," said Lil' Wolf, "Henry said I must come, I am his friend."

"Good Bye, my friends, we will see you at the 'Big Event'." Said Lil' Wolf, as he walked his pony into the forest.

Bud and I.J. dismounted and walked into the marshy area of the forest. They expected to have their limit of Marsh Hens and Drakes in a couple of hours. They always moved away from the younger men, who were too noisy for hunting, they claimed.

Henry and Charlie waved goodbye as Jimmy went to find a stand for himself and his gun. He will have the first shot, and the first kill. Thought Henry, he always did.

All of a sudden birds flew up into the blue sky and hurried away, and then Henry and Charlie heard a loud painful yell that echoed on the air, for many miles.

Henry went to get Justice, Charlie pulled on Mooney's bridle as he jumped onto the saddle in one jump. Henry was not too far from Charlie when he heard a second gut retching yell of pain he had not heard in a very long time.

Henry jumped on Justice's back just as Lil' Wolf rode in, wild and hard, into the clearing of woods he, Charlie, and Jimmie were hunting in.

Deer in the Woods

"What is it my friend?" Asked Henry, as he turned Justice to face Lil' Wolf.

"My Father, Big Chief, has been caught in a bear trap. Come, quickly, follow me, please Henry, he is an old man. Plenty Pain, Plenty Blood." Yelled Lil' Wolf as he turned his little Paint in the direction he came from.

"Charlie, quick get my bag from the front porch at the farm, Please hurry!" Begged Henry.

"Uncle Jim, will you come with me? Do you have your whiskey flask in your Hunting Jacket?" Asked Henry.

"Yes, Henry, I guess Aunt Fran put it in there, I didn't think of it. I'm ready lead the way. Follow Lil' Wolf, hurry before he gets out of sight!"

Henry and Jimmie kicked their horses to make them run a little faster through the woods. Lil' Wolf knew the woods better than they did and they didn't want him to leave them behind.

Lil' Wolf soon pulled up on his bridle of his pony and jumped off and ran to a man on the ground in front of him.

The Chief had passed out and could not feel the pain for a few minutes, giving Charlie time to get Henry's medical bag from the porch of Idle Wile'.

Henry and Jimmie reached Lil' Wolf just as he bent down over his father, who was in great pain, just as he came out of the faint he had passed into.

Jimmie grabbed a round hard branch as he ran toward the Tribal Chief of the Chitimacha Tribe, and Lil' Wolf's side.

Lil' Wolf knew why Jimmy had the heavy branch; he grabbed another under the old oak tree where the Chief had walked onto the huge trap.

Henry grabbed the whiskey flask from Jimmy and went to the head of the Chief, while opening the screw top of the flask. He poured a little into the top of the flask and put it slowly to the Chief's lips, giving him the time he needed to recognize who was kneeling next to his head.

"Oh, Yes," Said the Chief, through his pain. Henry slowly lifted the Chief's head, cradling it on his elbow, while balancing the small sip of whiskey he was slowly moving toward the Chief's lips. He opened his mouth just as Henry dipped the cap of whiskey. His eyes were filled with pain, but the whiskey calmed him down.

"Lil' Wolf moved toward his father's side, but Henry signaled him back to help Jimmie with the giant, strong bear trap.

Jimmie shoved the thick stick inside the bear trap without touching the Chief's foot or leg. He bore down on the stick as he pointed directions to Lil' Wolf to hold his stick in between the traps jaws. Lil' Wolf moved his stick further and further in between the teeth until Jimmie had unlocked the jaws of the trap.

The Chief lay back down on his shoulders and head in a low groan of hard pain.

Henry poured another cap full of whiskey and administered it, while the Chief's wet, red eyes, gave a grateful look toward Henry's fingers holding the cap of whiskey.

Charlie jumped off Mooney and ran to Henry's side with the black satchel of medicine. He had the satchel opened by the time he reached Henry.

Charlie pulled the bottle of Ether from the bag and reached in his back pocket for a clean white handkerchief to use as a cloth to hold the drops of Ether on it, as he gently closed the chief's eyes before covering his nose and face with the rag, to put the Chief to sleep.

The bear trap was still on the Chief's foot, even though the strong sticks were holding them away from the flesh by Jimmie and Lil' Wolf.

As soon as the Chief was soundly passed-out of his misery, Henry checked him to make sure he was well under the influence of the Ether, and doing its job, well. He looked at Jimmie and Lil' Wolf to remove the bear trap from the flesh and bone of the Chief's foot and leg.

"What a Mess!" said Charlie, "Who-ever set that trap here in these private woods is a criminal for sure."

Henry cleaned the awful wounds with Alcohol and quickly stitched the big and little holes made by the trap, as quickly and skillfully as he could, while Charlie pinched the flesh together. The bleeding ebbed.

Henry made the Sign of The Cross on Charlie, The Chief, and Himself, Thanking God. Jimmy did the same for himself and Lil' Wolf.

"You are so right, Charlie." Answered Henry, as he was bandaging the leg and foot of the Chief.

"Lil' Wolf, I will send el Rico to the village tomorrow to give the Chief another dose of Ether and a mixture of medicine to help the wounds heal. He can have a little whiskey, a little, listen to me good! Give him A Sip or Two to calm him down every three or four hours, as you can see that he needs it. No More!"

"Don't give the whiskey to anyone else at the camp. It drives them crazy, just like the Biloxi Indian Tribe, ok, Lil' Wolf?" asked Henry of his young and dear friend.

"I understand perfectly well." said Lil' Wolf. Making his sign from his heart to his head, which means, I promise. "I will go to my camp and get the Braves to bring a cradle bed to carry him back to the camp."

"Lil Wolf, no need to leave. Uncle Jimmie went to the farm to do just that, after you and he got the bear trap off your Father's foot and leg. They will be here shortly." Said Henry.

el Rico, and three other men from the farm came into the clearing where Henry, Charlie, and Lil' Wolf were caring for the Chief. They were carrying a bed made of thick straight branches and a canvas cradle set up between them.

"Charlie told us what happened to the Chief of the Chitimacha Tribe here in the woods! How can this happen?" asked el Rico.

"We don't know, yet. But we aim to find out. Me and Charlie are going into town the first thing this morning to find Jay and tell him what happened. I hope he is well from his own experience in the woods. I know Sheriff Ernest will be told also, so that's two of the best Law Men in this Country. It will not take long until we know who the vermin's who have done this are." answered Henry, as he made sure the Chief was comfortable and safe on the bed he would be carried to the village on to be taken care of by his people until he is well again.

Thank God for Henry's skills, patience, and understanding and medical knowledge, to take care of his patients and his people as well.

Henry told Lil' Wolf goodbye, to take care of himself, his Father and his Tribe, until the people who did this were found and punished for this horrible act of violence in the woods, where they all live and hunt.

Henry, Charlie and the rest of the family, and friends, returned to the farm. They are very quiet and somber. They are all looking forward to a hot bath, a good meal, and a drink and the Rosary on the porch before time to say 'Good Night' to family and friends.

"Charlie, I sure am glad the rest of the family is not here to experience this tragedy of the Chief of the Chitimacha. How sad this day has turned out to be. Good Night. Good friend." Said Henry. Good Night, Dear Friends.

Chapter Seventeen

"THE DAY BEFORE"

Bailey, Ethel M.T.

Henry and Charlie were back in New Orleans with the rest of the Family.

The Wedding is at mid-night Mass on Friday evening. Just two more days left on the calendar. Josh, Henry, and the Family had to be at the St. Lewis Cathedral at Eleven-Thirty; in the evening just a half hour before the Mass begins.

Josh was going to Confession, for the first time before his First Holy Communion, today, Thursday, only one more day before Christmas Eve.

Father Theriot was hearing Confessions at 11:00 A.M., Thursday, for Josh, The Parish, and for other Catholics who wanted to have Father hear their confession before Christmas Eve Mass.

Henry, Josh, Katherine, Louisa', Charlie, and the rest of the families, were taking advantage of this time for confession to all go with Josh and the Wedding Party. So the rest of the family came into town a day or two early to go to the Sacrament of Confession and visit and talk about the big plans happening in New Orleans, and eat the great foods the city is famous for.

The children were so excited. Uncle Henry and Charlie were taking them for a street car ride up and down the rail-line.

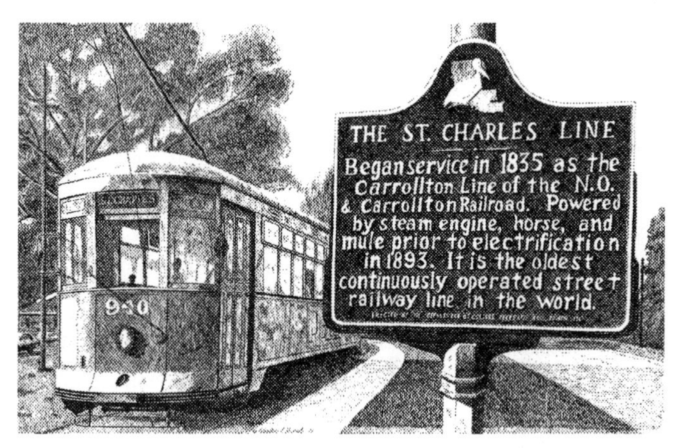

The Street Car

They would stop at the Zoo and go to lunch in the French Quarters. Charlie wanted to add the Museum to this list of things the children should see, today. The buildings were next to the Cathedral. How exciting to be in this beautiful city at this time of year. All the Christmas decorations were up on the houses, big and small. The city lamps were also decorated; the trees were smothered with icicles and the streets were lit by flam-bows. (Iron Flame torches, held in wall brackets. Each had a male Tender, taking care of it.) Each Business was decorated as well.

Henry and Charlie took the children to The Gumbo/Poor Boy Restaurant on the corner of Royal Street and Jackson Square for lunch. What a delight, and as the children learned that day. L.S.U., and Loyola, College Baseball Teams ate there too. WOW! What a day.

The children were all yawning, during the Street Car ride to St. Charles Avenue. "They are all tired, Charlie," Said Henry," we wore them out, all twelve of them".

"Yes," said Charlie, "we wore me out too".

"Me too," laughed Henry as the street car stopped in front of Henry's house. Charlie jumped off the car to help the children down the step. Henry asked him 'if he wanted to stay for a glass of wine or coffee and visit with the grown-ups for a while.'

"Henry, if I can make it up these steps, back onto the street car, I'm going home for some milk and a long nap." Laughed Charlie.

"Ok, Charlie, hope you don't miss a visit from Louisa'." Teased Henry.

"I'll be back, soon." Grinned Charlie, flicking the brim of his hat at Henry.

"Bye, Charlie, thanks for coming with me and the children, today. They really had a treat, especially Josh. He got all the attention, well almost. Madeline and Bella always get their share."

Katherine and Louisa' were showing off their new clothes from the New York shopping trip to their friends, who came to tea. Louisa' was showing her light-blue Bride Maids dress as well.

Katherine had asked Ms. Amy and Henry if Josh could wear a white velvet suit for his Baptism. She wanted to buy his suit, shoes and long socks and short gloves, and a box of small horses, for his big event. Henry said, "Sure honey, he would love all that attention and handsome clothes." She purchased it while in New York. Katherine's girlfriends enjoyed looking at Josh's clothes as well.

Ms. Jane picked up the boxes with Josh's new clothes when she left to go to Amy's house for coffee and cake. Ms. Bennett would be there also.

Jane arrived at the same time as Ms. Bennett. Amy met the ladies on the porch and called to Ms Bessie to bring in the coffee and cakes for the company.

Ms. Bennett had a request from Father Theriot concerning the flowers overflowing on the aisles of the church and the altar. His concern was that someone would trip over the trailing vines and would cause an accident. He asked Ms. Bennett to have them moved closer to the walls of the church.

Ms. Bennett said, "not to worry, she would use smaller vases and cut the flowers a little shorter, no one would know the difference".

The ladies were having their coffee and cake, when the Street Car stopped across the track by the house. Charlie and Henry helped the children get off the car and el Rico had crossed the street to help the children cross over to the sidewalk of the house.

"What tired babies they seem to be." said Amy. "Thank you el Rico, please take them inside to the Nannies, for a bath and a small treat before their naps."

"Did you have a good time riding the street car with Uncle Henry and Charlie?" Asked Ms. Jane.

The children all began to talk at once. "Babble, babble, babble."

"Oh, my goodness," said Ms Jane. "Wrong question! We will hear your stories, one at the time, at another time!" She and the other ladies, laughed, at the children's expressions.

"Run along now and get your baths and treats and a sound nap. You look very tired, but happy." Smiled Amy, as the children shook their heads in agreement.

el Rico shooed the children inside and on to the back of the house where the Nannies were waiting for their charges to return home, tired and happy, they were right.

Chapter Eighteen

"CHRISTMAS EVE MASS"

Bailey, Ethel M.T.

The Arrington Family and the Williams Family arrived at the Cathedral at Eleven O'clock, SHARP. Josh and Henry were too nervous to stay a minute longer at the house. So everyone in the two households was packed up and went to church.

Mid-night Mass in the St. Louis Cathedral was always sung by the Voices of the Opera Company of New Orleans. The Christmas Music began at Eleven – Thirty P.M

The front pews, on both sides of the Cathedral were reserved for the Baptismal and Wedding Parties. Good thing too, thought Henry, the Beautiful old Church was almost full when they arrived with two buggies and a Limousine full of people, dressed for the occasion.

St. Louis Cathedral

The Bride and Bridal Party, the girls, and Mother and Father of the Bride, were following the Usurer into the bridal rooms at the front of the church reserved for such occasions.

Henry, Josh and the Arrington family and friends, dipped the tips of their fingers in Holy Water, and made the Sign of the Cross. They genuflected by the front pew before they entered to be seated. First they kneeled to say a prayer to Jesus. Then they sat in the pew.

The Grooms family was seated on the Left hand side of the center aisle, while Katherine's families were on the right, and they were repeating the same Holy Rites of the Church.

At Mid-Night, the choir sang the Ave' Marie 'a.

Father Theriot and Thomas and other Altar Boys were making the Procession down the Center Aisle, following The Christ of The Cross and The Holy Bible and large White, lite Candles. Mid-Night Mass has begun.

Father began the Mass. After the Readings, Father motioned for Henry, Madeline, and Josh to join Him on the Altar. They were then introduced to the Congregation and received a grand applause, which surprised Josh and pleased him.

Father proceeded with the Sacraments of Baptism for Josh, with Henry and Madeline attending as God Parents. Father Theriot proceeded with Josh's First Holy Communion, as well. Josh was well blessed. He returned to his seat by Madeline and the other children. The Angels were singing.

Father Theriot continued with the Mass and Holy Communion. Josh received this Sacrament with the rest of His family and friends.

Father than motioned for Henry to join him on the Altar. The time had come during the Mass when Katherine and Henry would be Wed.

Henry and Charlie walked up to the Altar and stood on the Right side of the Center Aisle.

The beautiful Choir of the St. Louis Cathedral began the Wedding March. The Congregation stood up as the Wedding March began.

Father faced the congregation and smiled at Louisa', who was waiting for his sign to begin the Slow-Walk down the aisle, following Bella the Flower Girl, and Noah the Ring Bearer,. Followed by Louisa', Madeline and the Bridesmaids.

Then the Father of the Bride, Mr. Kurt and the beautiful Katherine, the Bride, followed the procession down the aisle to where Henry and Charlie were standing. Both as nervous as 'Cats'.

Charlie met Louisa' at the foot of the Altar, as Mr. Kurt's kissed Katherine on the cheek. "Don't go too Far, Daughter," He whispered in her ear. "I won't Dad." Katherine answered.

She then went to Join Henry, who was waiting for her.

The Ceremony went on, and then Father Theriot, said the magical words.

"I now pronounce you Man and Wife, Henry; you may kiss your Bride." Henry did.

They then returned to Henry's Pew to join the Family until the end of the Holy Mass.

"Mass is Ended, Go In Peace, Merry Christmas." Father said.

The Choir starting the Music and the Singing of 'Silent Night, Holy Night, all is clear all is"

Father and the Altar Boys lead the Procession, once more, down the aisle, carrying the Holy Cross of Jesus Crist the King, The Holy Bible and the Candles down the aisle with Henry, Katherine, and the Wedding Party followed by Josh and the families.

The rest of the Congregation was right behind the family and friends.

After Congratulations were given and received by the Happy Couple, everyone was looking for their buggies and cars to pick them up to go on to the Wedding and Josh's reception.

It was very cold and late, thought Amy.

Father was standing by the Great Open Doors of the Cathedral and Wishing and Receiving Christmas Greetings from HIs Flock, who was emerging from the Church.

Katherine and Henry were the first to Congratulate Father on The Ceremony of a Christmas Eve Mass, a Baptism, First Communion, and Wedding; he Superbly Blessed them with their Vows and the Congregations' Service.

Henry Handed Father a Blue Envelope with his and the family's Expression of Appreciation of Fathers' Superb Catholic Holy Ritual, for The Birth of Jesus and the Holy Sacraments' He Blessed Henry's family and the Congregation.

The Limousine picked up the Wedding Party and both Families to Ride to the Reception.

Chapter Nineteen

"THE RECEPTION"
(Le Bon Voyage)

Bailey, Ethel M.T.

The Buggies were waiting at the door of the Church, to pick up the people swarming out of the doors of the big Cathedral, at Two O'clock in the Morning.

All were headed to the Arlington Hotel on the River.

What a sight at such an hour on Christmas Morning, that is.'

There was almost a traffic jam on Canal Street, as the buggies were trying to see 'who got there first'. I never can figure out why, mentioned Amy to Henry, who was holding onto her and Josh and Katherine.

"Katherine, I guess you want to go home and change, before we go to the Reception, honey?

Asked Henry.

"No, thanks Henry, Mother got us a room at the Arlington, to dress into 'Party Clothes', and Gloria and Daisy will pick up our Wedding clothes and bring them to the cleaners," Said Katherine.

The Limousine stopped in front of the Hotel and Henry and Katherine, and the rest of the families walked across the sidewalk into the Lobby of the Hotel.

"Wow! Thought Henry, He was Amazed with the decorations, while Katherine was dazzled with the Chandeliers' and shimmering- shine of the Hotel Stairway.

"The children and Amy came into the Hotel Lobby. The eyes of the children were looking in disbelief at the decorations and beautiful Christmas Trees, with presents arranged under them.

The Children followed Henry and Katherine into the Ball Room; it was just beautiful with Lanterns, Candles on every window and Crystal Chandelier's on the ceiling.

Katherine and Henry walked into the Ball-room and were surrounded by their Friends who had lots of good wishes for their future together and Josh for the Ceremonies they had witnessed for his young Life.

The band was beginning to play, Henry and Katherine favorite song. 'Let the Good Times Roll.' Not the Wedding March or a Romantic Wedding song. But to watch them dance to that song was so much fun.

The Children spotted the Punch and Cake Table and tried not to run across the floor, getting there.

Katherine took Henry's hand when he would have started another dance and pulled him across the floor to the Cake Table.

"I'll explain later, Henry, we need to move this Party along. Trust me," said Katherine.

The entire group of friends went to the Cake table along with the Bride and Groom. Any sign of Cake in the picture, was a good thing.

Louisa 'was there waiting for them, and she handed Katherine the Wedding Knife, all tied up with a beautiful white bow at the end of the blade.

"Katherine, cut the cake, no time for Small talk, Poppa said to hurry you guys up to the boat."

Whispered Louisa'.

"Tell Henry, Louisa', I'll cut the cake", answered Katherine as she sliced through the most beautiful cake she had ever seen.

Louisa' was whispering to Henry, while Katherine was trying to shove a big piece of cake into Henry's closed mouth

"What, What, Gulp", said Henry. "Hush Henry, just listen, Poppa got the tickets for the Queen Mary and your luggage is being loaded as we speak. el Rico and Sassy are unpacking and arranging your Stateroom, to be ready when you get there."

"Poppa is sending them with you and Katherine, to take care of you." Henry was grabbing for a glass of Champagne, Katherine had in her hand.

He swallowed it all, "Sorry, K. Would you like a glass?" Asked Henry.

"No, thanks Henry, we don't have time. Poppa bought the tickets for the Queen Mary Cruise and it sails tonight in three hours, we have to board in two hours and we have to change clothes and tell the family goodbye. See?" Asked Katherine.

"Poppa and Mama will explain to the guest at the party what has happened. We will make a 'Grand Exit', than Poppa and Charlie will drive us out with many fare-wells to one and all."

"Our Luggage," Poppa said, is on the Queen Mary, in our State Room, he knows the Captain."

"el Rico and Sassy have unpacked for us, by the way, they're coming with us, Poppa said."

Henry and Kathrine went to Amy and the family to say they're good-byes.

"Have a wonderful Honeymoon, and come home ready to work." Said a teary eyed Amy.

"Uncle Jimmie and Aunt Francis are bringing us home, at a decent hour, if there is one left tonight." Said Amy as she and the family kissed Henry and Katherine, Goodbye.

The Uncles drove Amy and the Children home to the St. Charles Ave. home, and kissed them all a very good night.

"Can I fix you a cup of Tea, or a glass of Milk?" Asked Amy.

"Thank you, but we are going home, Amy. We will see you in the morning."

Said Jimmy. "Good Night, family."

"Good Night Uncle." Said the family.

Amy, Josh, Madeline, Bella and Noah, were half asleep saying the last beads of their Rosary for the day that had been a wonderful Day and Thanking God, at the end of the day, is such a Pleasure.

Well, Katherine and Henry are on the Queen Mary, with el Rico and Sassy for at least two weeks.

The Uncles, Amy, and the children are back on the Farms of the Arrington Plantations.

The Sheriffs have captured the Bear Trappers and they are in Jail for a long time.

While Charlie, Amy, Jerome, and the children are wondering: 'Just when is Henry coming Home'?

Everyone is working and enjoying their Church Life, The Families, the Evening Rosary and Everybody and Everything Good, in this World.

Lil' Wolf's Father has recovered, even though he likes to pretend he still needs to be carried in the chair the Warriors and Lil' Wolf made for him. His father laughs all the time, for the love of life, God has given to him.

Lil' Wolf and the beautiful Maiden of the Stars were married with a wonderful night of Fires under the Moon, Stars, and Fireflies.

Maiden of the Stars

Lil' Wolf's guests were his new friends Father Theriot and the judge and also his Great Friends, the families of the Arrington Plantations and Charlie, Jay and Ernest.

Ms Bessie and Sassy made many cakes, pies, bread, and Root Beer.

Jerome smoked a side of beef for three days, it was perfection.

Josh, Noah, Ben, Bella, Madeline, and the cousins danced the dance of the Indian Tribe with the children of the Chitimacha Tribe. They were not too bad. They stomped their bare feet in the dirt and laughed a lot.

They all had a wonderful time.

Lil' Wolf and Star rode away into the forest on Warrior, into the night.

Them boys Josh, Ben, Noah, and the cousins spend their days dreaming of fishing and talking about the scary skull in the river bed. A lot of their time is spent shoveling around the pecan trees, picking pecans for pies and fudge, but mainly just looking for treasure (as they tell Amy and Ms. Bessie). The pecan trees have never looked so clean or produced so many pecans in a season.

Every once in a while, one of the boys will find a silver spoon or a china cup, but no treasure, and not all in one place. Oh well, umm, good luck boys.

"Just wait until Henry gets back, he can help us dig, and he's pretty smart. He will know where that old crinkly, dirty map is leading us to around this old plantation." Proclaimed Josh. Noah and Ben both agreed wholeheartedly.

The girls are perfecting their knitting and crocheting in the afternoon and enjoying being taught by Amy and Ms. Bessie on the their balcony, where they can watch the boys dig and clean all around those old pecan trees.

My Wish for you is that you enjoy reading this book as much as I enjoyed writing it.

"God Bless You!"

Thank You, Good Night Dear Friend. –Ethel Bailey

THE END

About the Author

Ethel M. T. Bailey grew up near New Orleans, Louisiana surrounded by plantations. She visits New Orleans regularly and loves the city, its heritage, and its culture. She still resides in south Louisiana and enjoys spending her time with her family. Her previous works include: "Le Petit Cajun Esprit" and "Lily Pond Village".

Printed in the United States
By Bookmasters